PERMANENT VACATION

THE ESCAPIST SERIES

CALLY RADUENZEL

Acknowledgments

No author gets the job done without help. Top o' the list is my partner in crime as in life Polly Jones. Thank you for putting up with my constant beefing, editing, ruminating, worrying, kvetching, blabbering, blubbering and dreaming about the birth and finally the publication of "Permanent Vacation". You remind me everyday that life is about enjoying the ride and not just the destination! I love you, sweetheart!

Liz Mason and Robin Bougie, for as busy as you both are running your own show, publishing your own masterpieces and working the "day jobs"…you both found a way to write such thoughtful reviews for the back of my book that will really direct the right reader to my lair! So many thanks!

Elizabeth Yellen I'm so glad I've been cutting your hair all these years, it really paid off! I needed an editor and there you were…like an angel during our COVID year. Some how we got a break from our lives and got to escape to a world not touched by that pesky virus.

Lisa Marie…girl, I know you had better things to do but it really helped that you went though the book from beginning to end right before I was ready to publish. You caught a lot of important stuff and I am grateful!

Lee Lewin thank you for giving me the push to write a second book. "Permanent Vacation" may have never happened without you.

BIG HUGE SHOUT OUT to Mitch O'Connell my cover artist who doesn't know me from a hill of beans and yet gave me this beautiful and bad ass cover to use for the price of a dream…c'mon readers, help me make a million so I can pay this tremendous talent!

Joe Allen Black without you it wouldn't look like a book! Graphic artist supreme!

Jennifer Meece, my dear cousin, best friend and soul sister- you've read all my stories that lead up to this one since we were reading Judy Blume and Dick Francis. You are such a blessing in my life, I really don't know what I'd do without you.

Bob Raduenzel, when you first told me you were moving to Hawaii I thought it was the end of the world. I was so broke and I thought I'd never see you again but low and behold Hawaii is what brought you so much closer then just being my brother. There's a lot of Neal in you but thankfully you have never been kidnapped by drug smugglers.

Cause I'm am home and I am staying this time
Home, home no more crying this time
I am home and I want you to know
That I'll never leave, I'll never go

-Henry Kapono/ Cecilio & Kapono
Album- Elua
Song- Home (And I'm Staying This Time)

"It's in the stillness that fills me with peace…"

-Tom Bodett, author of "The End of The Road"
***(He'll leave the light on for us)**

"I am sure most of the influences responsible for ones cast of mind are too remote and mysterious to be known, but I happen to know a few of the influences responsible for mine."

-Joseph Mitchell, "Up In The Old Hotel"

"You go away for a long time and return a different person—you never come all the way back."

Paul Theroux, "Dark Star Safari"

"In a half an hour the street would come to life again with cocktail traffic but now this very superior half mile of rich road …held nothing but the suspense of an empty stage and the heavy perfume of a night-scented jasmine."

Ian Fleming, "Doctor No"

"The truth in the beginning , the star of the show was Hawaii, next was the red Ferrari and then it was Selleck."

Larry Manetti, "Aloha Magnum,"

"Let me say at the top that I didn't have a particularly good reason for going…I was simply restless…because of the dissatisfaction …of my life…"

-J. Maarten Troost, "The Sex Lives of Cannibals

Prologue

When she looked out the lodge window at the impending autumn of Fossil Creek, with its early morning mist off the lake and a lonely fishing boat floating in the distance, she realized how comforting her adopted small town had become. This urban champion from Chicago had settled into a quaint small-town lifestyle and for a while it was her oasis from the world.

Now, with the sudden death of her dad, she was feeling an old itch. She was restless. She needed to see her brother and get out of her life for a bit.

Her phone had been buzzing up a storm even though she'd put it on silent. It was work. It was always work.

Things at the hair salon she owned, things that normally wouldn't annoy her, now set her off to the point where she was ready to snap. This wasn't Lucy—Lucy was always someone who laughed easily and was heavy on the charm, "a hardworking Norwegian," her grandpa used to say with a pat on her shoulder, as he ruffled her curly blond hair. But lately it was all tension, curse words, and annoyances. She attempted to resume redecorating her home "office."

Amanda, her partner, had examined all the unpacked boxes. "It's gonna look like a Tiki Bar threw up in here," she commented comically as she stood shaking her head, hands on her hips, in a pair of cargo shorts and Montreal Canadiens hockey jersey, before calling it a night.

"World traveler, exotica . . . that's my vibe," Lucy theatrically corrected Amanda. On second thought . . . it was heavy on the Hawaiian bar wear and rattan furniture. She smiled as she gazed on the huge pièce de résistance of her mounting collection, a chandelier made of taxidermied puffer fish that she had bought it on auction back in Chicago at an estate sale. It somehow felt extra exotic in the wiles of Canada!

When Lucy had acquired this former Canadian lodge, it had been neglected and in rough shape. The "Great Room," as she liked to call it, was formerly part of a front desk check-in sitting area with a huge picture window looking out onto Lac De Lune.

Cracked linoleum and a wobbly wood-paneled check-in desk that smelled like must and moth balls had been torn out and was now a cozy sitting area filled with a mixture of Tommy Bahama's Island Estate furniture, which looked more Kenyan safari and less hunting shack. The gold stained shag carpeting with cigarette burns and mystery goo matting it down by the seating area had been removed and replaced with the thick plush animal skins found in storage from years before, when the place had truly been a hunting lodge. All this rustic decorating added to the integrity of the lodge's outdoorsy surroundings without looking so dumpy and forlorn. Lucy was a reader, so lots of dark-wood bookcases complemented the lodge's expansive walls. She even had a shrunken head—that she'd picked up at a "Cabinet of Curiosities" collectors' event on a wharf in Seattle. This was her freaky little oasis from the world and she loved it!

"Lucy, your phone is ringing again," Amanda called out from the bathroom. It was late and she was sick of talking to work and answering the never-ending texts.

Amanda added, "Don't forget I'm helping Bob out at the store tomorrow."

"OK," she yelled back. "I'm just gonna load a few more things onto the shelves and I'll meet you in the hot tub!"

Lucy flipped on some West Coast jazz and began cleaning up her mess of boxes and packing material. Stan Getz and Chico Hamilton always relaxed her and helped her wind down.

Quickly she ran and got her phone, texted her response, and plunked down in the middle of her towers of books. "I need to get the hell out of here."

It was a year or more since her last vacation and she was *crispy*. Her life had been a whirlwind of massive changes, mostly for the good, but modern life had snuck into the out-of-the-way little town. Taking over the hair salon and flipping it into a "destination" was a total surprise, but the escape that brought her from Chicago to Fossil Creek, Canada, now made her want to feel the island breeze on her face and throw her phone overboard.

Amanda kept reminding her that all she had to do was book a flight to her brother's in Oahu and she could exhale and relax, but she hadn't pulled the trigger . . . maybe it was time.

Lucy and Amanda had met auspiciously almost two years before. Amanda was a reclusive "mountain woman" type living on Lucy's recently deceased uncle's property in a cottage that was now her writing studio. Amanda had been the caretaker for Lucy's uncle's property. Lucy at first thought she was kind of an asshole, with her snappy comments and flippant comebacks, but after their initial rough start, Cupid's arrow had hit swiftly and Amanda and Lucy had been inseparable ever since . . . sort of.

One thing about two strong-willed women is . . . *they are both strong-willed women,* and both Lucy and Amanda had their own lives. But since their marriage in Hyannis, Massachusetts, they'd both bloomed into the people they both desired to be: Lucy becoming a successful businesswoman with her hair salon and band and Amanda becoming more social and part of the community she loved so much, while still editing coffee-table books for a company in Montreal.

Amanda's latest "side hustle" had become helping Bob, their mutual friend, run his ever-popular general store and restore old motorcycles.

Fossil Creek, their remote winter retreat town, had become a tourist hot spot ever since Rick Steves, a famous travel author, had blogged about their "enchanted village hidden in plain sight" right outside of Montreal. Now on any given day the big stuffed moose in Bob's storefront window was photographed more than a supermodel in Milan.

So with all this good fortune why was Lucy feeling so irritable and discontent?

Her phone glowed yet again with an incoming text. "Cops are at the salon, silent alarm went off—please advise." It was 11:30 at night and she was in sweats looking like a slob. She texted back, "Well, did anyone break in?"

"Yes," was all her manager could text back. So now she was on the way over to check the damage.

She would call her brother tomorrow and book the flight. It was time to go rogue. She was ready for a little aloha.

Chapter 1

February in Hawaii couldn't come fast enough.

Since Lucy had purchased the Hair Hut, now renamed Tout Le Monde Salon, the business had morphed from the tiny mom-and-pop beauty shop to a full-service grooming parlor and salon.

Lucy's original fantasy of a relaxed, less urban life had become a whirlwind of accommodating all kinds of clients seven days a week. The locals still wanted that intimate, not-too-fancy feel, so she had kept the main room more rustic and actually had added hot lather straight-razor shaves for all the loggers, fisherman, and outdoors-men who were the backbone of the town's industry. Then she had amped up the "ladies'" services for a fancier feel. Randy, her buddy and fellow hairstylist, helped run the business, while Amanda did the bookkeeping. Between the lodge and the salon they also had music events on the first and fourth Fridays of the month.

Her family attorney had exclaimed in a drunken moment of oversharing, "You Zwick kids sure know how to fall in shit and come out smelling like roses," referring to her and her brother's mix of bad luck and good luck. Lucy had inherited the lovely winter lodge only to have her dad die the following Christmas and her best friend since first grade, Crystal, pass away six months later—this series of events seemed to be typical of the paradoxes in her and her brother's lives.

Two years ago Lucy had thought her life was falling apart, then she moved to Fossil Creek and it was magical. The town was full of lovely people and she'd found the love of her life! She kept waiting for something bad to happen but it didn't!

Then her musical ambitions came full circle and her new band had been signed by a record label. It was all happening! But that dream unraveled when the music company closed down. So she tromped on, cutting hair and building her business and learning to be Amanda's life partner.

What was the next step? Amanda was encouraging her to go to Hawaii. "I think you are snippy and short tempered because you need to clear your head. You've had quite the roller coaster going on in your life. I'm not trying to be a jerk, but we can handle the load here. You always say Hawaii is your medicine." Amanda made this suggestion strongly—she always had a no-nonsense way of figuring things out.

Lucy knew Amanda was right and tried not to be defensive. Somehow, she knew there was something more for her to do, and it wasn't just her next corrective color or haircut.

She found a listing for a monthlong "live-a-board" on a Cigale sixteen-foot sailboat, docked at **La Mariana Sailing Club**. A Mr. Jimmie Jay Choi was looking for a responsible renter for his floating hotel room.

To live on a boat had been a fantasy for her since Jack Klugman played Quincy and lived aboard a sailboat on a slip in Marina del Rey, where he was wooing the ladies when he wasn't practicing forensic medicine. "Oh this is just what I'm looking for," she delighted, dialing his number.

Jimmie Jay Choi had a sort of happy, annoyed voice, slightly high pitched, the English-as-a-second-language variety. "Hiya, Jimmie Jay here." She could hear him burping beer all the way from Hawaii to Canada. Jimmie Jay sounded relaxed, even in his excitement. This appealed to her.

"Hi, I'm Lucy, answering your ad." She was sitting in her big leather Danish Modern desk chair that reminded her of a baseball glove. There were three feet of snow outside her window from a surprise snow squall that had hit out of nowhere. A light icy breeze was sneaking through the seal in her window, reminding her of just how cold it was outside.

"Ok, what choo want?" His tone now sounded like he had no idea what she was calling about.

"This is *the* Jimmie Jay Choi renting the boat for a month, right?" she double-checked the printout of the advertisement.

"Why-eee, who wants to know?" Now his tone was nervous and suspicious.

"Well, I found your ad on Craigslist . . . and I would like to rent your boat while I'm there visiting my brother."

"Then I think you should give me your name and let me check you out. Lemme get a pen."

Lucy could hear him rummaging around, then the familiar Zippo flick, and Jimmie Jay inhaled deeply on a cigarette as the *scritch-scritch* of his pen took down her information.

"Um, ok, Lucy Zwick. I get back to you," he said flatly.

Lucy then added, "I'm a musician . . . and business owner . . . and I want to get away . . . and I thought a boat would be perfect for solitude and being close to the water."

She attempted to explain but he cut her off.

"I just don't want no freaky shit and I need to check you out, make sure you got money. I call you back in thirty minutes. You be there!" He commanded and then abruptly hung up.

"What the fuck?" She shook her head, holding the phone. This guy sounded like a real piece of work.

She watched Combover, her English bulldog, snore soundly at her feet, while she waited for her call back from Mr. Jimmie. She petted Combover's wrinkled brow, feeling guilty she couldn't take him with her—he would have been the perfect companion.

Lucy looked at her phone as she sat in her home office—a smartphone is a dangerous time eater, but also afforded her time to run a tight business even when she wasn't on-site. It also made her on call 24/7. Randy was texting her and she appreciated his attention to detail but there were times she wished he would just keep control of the zoo and not bug her for every little thing.

He was busy fixing the broken window from the other night when kids had broken in to try and steal the cash box. They did mostly credit card business so the kids made off with less then a hundred bucks and got busted trying to buy a case of Molsen at Big Bob's Convenience Store. Randy wanted her to know the work had been completed and the kids parents were paying for the damage.

She thanked Randy just as her phone rang with an 808 exchange. She picked up on the first ring. "Dis' Lucy," Jimmie Jay said, sounding a bit more congenial.

"It's me!" She tried to sound comical and yet responsible. "I wanted to check you out, so we have no funny business but you got to know I'm not a licensed rental. I was a Honolulu cop, *retired.*" He paused to let that fact sink in. "Last time I go out of town they was filming a porno on my boat deck . . . almost lost my slip, then I got nowhere to park this thing, ya know."

Lucy laughed. "Porno, huh! Ya spoiled all my big plans."

"Yeaaaa. I wasn't in it! Haha, or maybe I would've been a little happier," he laughed. "See, the thing is, Miss Lucy, we not supposed to do live-a-boards at this sailing club, but lots of people do . . . you just gotta be cool, not make a spectacle. . . ." He paused. It sounded like he was still drinking beer even though it was only at 10 a.m. Honolulu time. "Now, I don't charge a crazy big fee, but I require a big deposit. As long as you don't trash my boat, we're all good. OK. No negotiating here." He was quiet again, letting that sink in.

"Sounds good, Jimmie." She was so excited the butterflies in her stomach made her feel like a little kid on Christmas. They hung up both feeling good about the transaction. She had her own curiosities, like how did a former cop/bartender afford such a nice yacht. But she wasn't into playing detective.

Amanda wasn't able to get off work for the Hawaii trip, which was just as well—she wasn't really a boat person. "If you need me, Lucy, I'm just a phone call away," Amanda offered.

Randy also cut hair and had given Amanda a new look. Her short, cropped blond hair was much more wash-and-wear, and tucked under her favorite floppy wool ski hat, she looked very Swiss Alps chic.

Lucy felt guilty, talking a mile a minute as they pulled into the airport terminal.
"I will let you know all the scoop and try and give you a daily rundown!" Lucy said.

"Honey, it's a vacation not a business trip, call when you feel like it. I'm a big girl. I don't need you to check in, unless you want to!" Amanda laughed, going in for a big bear hug and smooch as they stood in front of the icy terminal.

Lucy was already fantasizing about blue skies, the Pacific Ocean, and her brother's cooking. Good-bye, snowstorm—it was Mahalo time!

Chapter Two

Neil knew shit was going to be fucked up when he drove up the endless driveway to the Yellow Mansion.

He put his Land Cruiser in park and paused. He didn't want to get wrapped up in a fuckin' domestic dispute. What was he, a cop? *Jesus* . . . he was a trader and beach bum, just the way he liked it!

Then he heard two gun shots go off.
"Oh, no, not today, motherfucker," he cursed to himself. His sister was coming in from Canada—he did not need this shit. He got his gun from the glove compartment and checked it. Loaded. He probably shouldn't take it but Gabe's wife was a nut job and loved fuckin' guns.

He checked his phone and saw a text: "ETA???" It was Gabe again.
"I'm here," Neil answered.

Gabe typed: "Ocean side . . . she's swinging her dick. . . so announce yourself."

Neil was already out of the car. Halfway around the house he could see them on the patio—too much money and not enough good sense. He could tell Gabe was high, pacing back and forth, and Debbie had that damn diamond-encrusted Ruger LCR, little but lethal. Those two idiots belonged together!

He hid behind the tall imported bushes for a few minutes to get a take on things.

"You screwed our daughter's best friend, you little weasel. Did you put some coke up her nose too?"

Neil cringed. *Oh . . . not good . . .*

Gabe looked sweaty in his madras preppy shirt circa 1980s. "It just fuckin' happened, I told you. I was drunk . . . she was coming on to me. I took care of it. I'm so, so sorry."

Debbie shot the Ruger with scary precision aim at the beach ball right next to Gabe, who was on the lawn chair. The ball exploded into smithereens. "Lies, your theme song should be 'Liar'!" she screamed. Neil could see spit flying out of her mouth.

He picked his moment then. He called out and shook his arms in the air like a goofy gorilla. "Guys, guys, guys, what is going on here?" He came out of the bushes like a stumbling Rodney Dangerfield trying to ward off the mob after a bad night at the track.

Debbie adored Neil, and that's why Gabe had called him.

"This motherfucker screwed Lisa's best friend. He's a fuckin' pig, Neil—she's barely seventeen."

Neil was six foot eight and an imposing, bald, Mr. Clean-looking kind of guy, but his good-natured manner made him a charmer and he knew how to play the game.

"Gabe, what the *fuck,* man." He shook his head like he was agreeing with Gabe's wife.

Gabe responded, "I know, it's fucked up. I know. I don't know what I was thinking."

Good call, Neil thought, be repetitive. Show remorse. "Debbie, it looks like Gabe knows he really messed up. Let's put the gun down. Let me get you a drink. Here," he pulled out a chair for her, patted the seat, and walked over to the bar. "You still like Johnny neat, water back?"

She sighed deeply. "Yeah, that sounds good. Make it a double."

Neil poured the drink and placed the tumbler in front of Debbie.

Gabe was an idiot. Debbie was a smoking hot babe—she used to model for La Perla lingerie, she was classy and spoke three languages, and there wasn't one ounce of silicon in her. And he's gotta go chasing some teenager. This was why Neil didn't like having friends. Too many problems.

"Gabe, come over here and sit your ass down," Neil ordered, pulling another chair across from Debbie for him to park it. Neil sat between them, pouring himself three fingers of his favorite whiskey.

"This is not the way to fix shit. Debbie, the gun is never a good idea. *And Gabe,* I think you need to suck it up and go see the therapist with her. I don't think she's asking too much . . . *do you, Gabe*?"

Gabe shook his overly gelled thick head of dark hair. "No, no, I see, it's gone too far."

"Gabe, you want to make this right for Debbie, right?" Neil said, almost sternly.

Debbie was nodding, and she took a deep swig of her Johnny Red.

Gabe agreed, "Yes, she's the only woman I have ever loved. I don't know what happened. I'm an idiot."

"Yes, you fuckin' are, Gabe," Debbie agreed, letting him feel the grill under the hot seat.

Neil kicked back his final gulp of Johnny Red. "Now, I love you both. I don't want to bury anyone or be bailing either of you out, but I need to go pick up my sister from the airport."

"Oh my God," they said in unison, "That's great! You gotta bring her by!"

Just like that the Henning's were back.

He reached over and hugged them both. He began getting up, pushing his chair back under the patio table. "Now, don't get drunk and start this shit all over again, OK? Debbie, go stay at your sister's. And Gabe, you just stay here and think about what you've done."

Neil almost snickered—he sounded just like his stepmother.

"OK, that's a good idea," Debbie said. "Can you drop me off?"

Gabe gave Neil a pleading look.

Neil nodded. "Sure, but make it fast."

"Thanks Neil," Debbie said scooting into the house.

True to her word, they were on the road in minutes.

Debbie's sister lived was in a condo overlooking Waikiki Beach. On the drive to *literally* the most expensive condo building in Oahu, Neil gave Debbie some support and listened to her vent. By the time they arrived at The Residences at the Mandarin Oriental she was laughing and patting his knee.

"Jenny is lucky to have you, Neil. I hope some of you rubs off on Gabe. He needs to lay off the blow—he always does dumb shit when he's putting that up his nose."

"I would agree."

The parking attendant gave Neil a thumbs-up, mistakenly thinking Debbie was his arm candy.

He winked and shook his head no and pulled away. Just then his phone rang.

"Neil, I'm stuck on the side of the road and some gangbanger is trying to help me fix my car."

Neil pulled and U-ey and called his sister. "Hey, when you get off the plane I won't be there. Jenny had car problems. I'll meet ya at the boat. Text me the address."

"What a fuckin' day," he said, shaking his head and getting on the H1.

CHAPTER 3

The thing Lucy really liked about Oahu was how little it seemed to change. The airport, the swaying palm trees, Kahuku Superette for Poke, La Mariana Sailing Club in Honolulu for pupus and cocktails.

She could spend a day watching the yachts come in and out among the thick green enchanted fronds and dark port waters of the harbor. The locals were usually good-natured and chipper.

Ted's carrot cake, always moist, and Kalua Pig Nachos, smoky and dripping with hot cheese and spice—ahhh yes, that's the stuff! The concrete high rises that still had that 1970s vibe shared their space with newer architecture, cell phones, and congestion.

Honolulu restaurants may have evolved into the upscale mainstream tapestry, but much of the aloha soul held on to its roots with a seemingly breezy vise grip. Travelers just had to venture outside of the big city to feel Oahu's own island culture. Real Hawaiians weren't hanging out in Waikiki—just ask Willie K, a singing musical treasure.

Before her trip to visit her brother in Oahu she'd been loading up on all the Hawaiian kitsch. Watching *Hawaii Five-0* classic and comparing it to the more recent remake of *Hawaii Five-0* (she loved both). Then there was her favorite retro TV show, *Magnum P.I.* Lucy knew the streets of Kalanianaole Highway, where the fictional "Robin's Nest" island retreat of Robin Masters was located. The property was still there but owned by someone new who was rehabbing the Waimanalo Beach property.

There were the restaurants like Crouching Lion on the North Shore, close to her brother, that overlooked the ocean but it had recently closed so the "party" had moved to "**Seven Brothers**" further down the road. There was a great group of locals who frequented the restaurant for late-night eats the **Paniolo Cowboy Burger** seemed to be the chow of choice with a special sauce and a fried onion ring under the hood of a sweet bread bun. They mostly maintained the integrity of who they had always been. Would it be the same on this visit? Lucy wondered, she hoped. The fast changes of the world and her life made her wonder if anything could survive this brutal modern world.

Lucy's brother always liked to pick her up at the airport, but his wife Jenny was having car issues and was stuck on the shoulder of the road by Pearl City, not the best area. Neil had to pick her up first, so Lucy decided to grab a cab.

Lucy took the cab to the dock where her boat was waiting. Her cab driver wasn't much of a talker, but they stopped at a Starbucks, and after an iced caramel macchiato, her treat, he helped her carry her bags to the boat.

Lucy got settled in her floating hotel room. The yacht was anything but palatial—it felt like a kid brother's bedroom with neon beer signs in the tiny windows over the bed bunk and kitchen galley. A calendar of sexy pinup babes on the minifridge and multicolored nautical floating balls with little lights inside them illuminated the small cabin space. The cabin included the combo bed/couch next to the multi-use kitchen table/wet bar/ desk. It was set up like an interior of a tiny RV. But when she climbed outside and stepped onto bow of the boat, it was a breathtaking island getaway. The lapping of the waves rocked the yacht ever so gently, and her new Top Sider boat shoes made her feel secure against the seemingly slippery fiberglass boat floor.

She sat down on one of the sturdy little deck chair seats and took in the view from her slip. Most of the neighboring boats were empty, and as the sun set many of the yachting types had made their way to the marina for cocktails and **pupus**, also known as appetizers. The breeze was sweet and reassuring, as though nothing could possibly be wrong in the world. No struggle, hunger, or strife could wreck this moment of bliss.

Until her cell phone's vibrating text notification scared the shit out of her. She jumped, shocked at the unwelcome intrusion. Heart pounding, she laughed, embarrassed, and looked around nervously to see if anyone had caught her freak-out. The docks seemed eerily empty.

The green cube on her iPhone showed two texts: one from her long-lost music agent Guy (pronounced *Gee*—he was French Canadian). He had been relatively MIA since the music recording contract had fallen through a year ago. Guy tried to get her some gigs but the money wasn't great for unknown acts who didn't play covers of popular songs recorded by famous bands. And it was a lot of work for her and her band, who already had day jobs and families, to practice weekly.

The text from Guy simply said CALL ME in capitals. The second text popped up saying, NOW. Given the six-hour time difference, she just texted back, GOOD TO HEAR FROM YOU, JUST ARRIVED IN HONOLULU, WILL CALL YOU IN TWO WEEKS WHEN I GET BACK.

Then she pressed "send" and cracked open a Diet Pepsi, and settled in to feel the waves gently rock her back and forth, as the orange and gold sun sank against the fading blue horizon like an electric tie dye.

She almost ruined her tranquility with bitter thoughts of dashed dreams of "rock stardom." Why did Guy have to text her right now, when she was trying to relax and forget real life for a minute?!

All her life that had been the dream, to become a famous singer. How did she let herself believe such a fantasy? Yet for a quick minute in her life, it seemed possible.

Lucy had tried to hold on after the music company went bankrupt. She knew her songs were good, they were catchy and meaningful—her band had gone the funky, soul route and it seemed so good, but they weren't a "bar band" churning out classic rock, or a hipster skinny jean and black eyeliner, fuzzed-out guitar band either. The long weekends when they drove through snowstorms to places where there was no heat, and breaking their backs packing up equipment in ice storms, was starting to wear them down. After some of their gear had been stolen she realized she had let that dream go. It happened quietly—she just stopped trying to book them; why was she holding on to something folks just weren't that into? Lucy's only consolation was that other musicians loved her band and so did bartenders. But when no one from the band complained about when the next gig was coming, she knew it was time to lay the music to rest. Lucy had thrown in the towel to focus on her salon, which thankfully was thriving.

Her phone buzzed again. Fuck, really?! she thought. She almost tossed her phone in the ocean.

The text from Guy said: CALL ME!

She had come here to get away from her life, not be reminded of past disappointments. She wasn't in the mood for some "birdseed" gigs from Guy. So she turned off her phone.

Her mind was racing. But before she could obsess she heard the big clomps of feet on the pier. It was her brother!

"Neil!" she shot up excitedly and raced to her big, six-foot-eight "little" brother.

"Just me," he bellowed, jumping aboard. "I dropped Jenny off back home. She's packing for her work trip."

Neil gave her a big bear hug and she almost started crying. It was just so good to see him. After Dad's passing and all the stress of seven days a week starting the salon just seeing him again reconnected her to herself. She had felt so alone in the world as if she was related to no one and had been left behind. These were all the things she told her brother over blue-cheese dip and a martini for him, a soda and lime for her, as the sun dissolved into its indigo island blanket for the night. Jimmie Jay had stocked the fridge for her and that really made the trip get off to a good start.

"Where is Jenny going?" Lucy asked as she started tidying up so they could go out for sushi.

"You know my scientist spouse. She's heading to the Kwajalein Islands to work on some government stuff. I think it actually has to do with cancer research, but I have no idea—she doesn't discuss work with me much. So I may go, just for a few days, if it's OK with you. She has to see if she can get clearance, ya know, no civilians without clearance."

Lucy was a little taken aback. She had thought this trip was all about Neil and her catching up. She was OK, she could use a little private time. Maybe catch up with her other friends on the island.

Then it occurred to Lucy that they were going to the same island her dad's sister and kids had lived on for quite a few years when her uncle worked for NASA. "Did Jenny ever meet Uncle Edwin, who worked on the space shuttle?" Lucy asked, locking the cabin door as they made their way out for dinner.

"Yes, they met once, but Jenny and I were still so young, she wasn't working back then. She was just a student. You know Uncle Edwin, he's not a big talker." Uncle Edwin had a habit of snapping the newspaper to attention and "reading the paper" in the center of a chaos-filled room as a way of removing himself from the family. Eccentrics don't always have blue spiked hair.

They headed to **Yanagi Sushi** on Kapiolani Boulevard. There was parking and it was her brother's favorite sushi joint in town. Supposedly all the well-connected Japanese folks came here for the best spider roll, sashimi, and **chicken katsu**.
Neil liked it because it opened early and kept late hours. He was always looking for intrigue, and allegedly from time to time some of the Asian underworld made its way to this place for dinner. Lucy's brother's life was quiet, so he liked to spice it up with stories from his neighbors.

They got seated and ordered. As Neil took a sip of his warm saki, he asked, "Are you gonna have a problem if I go on this thing with Jenny? I'd be back next Monday, so that still gives us lots of time."

"No, not at all, I want to do some 'Lucy' stuff, ya know, **Idea's Bookstore**, **Duke's brunch** with **Kapono** singing, that kinda stuff, I know you guys aren't into that."

Now it was his turn to grab his phone. "That's probably Jenny."

The waitress was serving their rolls as his face took on a perplexed look, "Luce, do you know a guy named *Guy*? He just texted me for you to call him. Oh, shit, Jenny's calling. I'm gonna grab it—"

Lucy said she'd be right back: "I'll call Guy, you call Jenny." Lucy could feel her blood begin to boil. *Texting my brother?* Seriously? The only reason Guy had her brother's phone number was from last year, when he was visiting Waikiki on vacation. *Can't take the hustle outta the hustler.*

The restaurant was loud, so Lucy had to go outside.

The phone barely rang twice. "Finally, Jesus, can't ya call me back," Guy said, sounding irritated.

"Well hello to you, too." Jesus, she thought, irritated, paradise interrupted already!

She could tell that he was excited. "I'm gonna make your dreams come true but I need you to commit tonight because they are considering another artist besides you."

Lucy didn't like the sound of this. All her rash decisions had gotten her in trouble in the past—why should this be any different?

"I told you if I could get your music in the right people's hands it would be off to the races! I came through for you, Lucy! They want to hire you to write for Ashly Martin. She's changing her image and wants to sing something more than contrite pop songs. They LOVE—and I mean love—your songs. It's a big payday and if the album does well, more songs, more money."

So there Lucy stood, in the parking lot with frantic Asians parking luxury cars, sweating in the hot Hawaiian night and trying to escape her life, but her life had followed her here. This could be the biggest decision she would ever make financially in her life and Amanda was back in Canada, while Todd, her bandmate and cofounder of the band, was in Saskatoon . . . and she was in shock. She weighed the facts over and over, she knew she needed to jump on this deal—her only key out of chaos.

Performing was a young person's gig, she reasoned. She could still create great music with Todd, and not have to worry about her ass size or cramming into a van and playing for a two-person crowd. Plus, the deal sounded like it had a future. So with a deep sigh, Lucy just said, "Yes."

Hopefully her writing partner Todd would understand. She lamented to Guy.

"Lucy, he already agreed. *He called me back*"—Guy cleared his throat—"right away, unlike you."

"Oh, well . . . OK then." Lucy paused. "Do you really think this is the right move?" she nervously wavered.

"If your songs can get famous by someone who's won more Grammy's than Taylor Swift, then I'd say you have a lot more leverage out there in radio-land to strike a deal for yourself. Look at Sia or Willie Nelson."

Lucy shifted her weight; the leather of her sandals was biting into her feet. Exhaling deeply as some guy spit not far from her bare foot, she had a lump in her throat. This was right, she felt it strongly.

Guy explained, ". . . long story short, I'm gonna send some files. Click on the yellow DocuSign boxes. It has your signature so you can just initial them, but I need them in the next couple of hours, OK?"

"I'll do it now, Guy." As Lucy spoke she signed her contracts, attempting to read the fine print on her little iPhone.

"So I'm gonna be the next Diane Warren," Lucy joked, feeling butterflies in her stomach. Diane Warren was one of Lucy's favorite pop song writers. She'd written for LeAnn Rimes, How Do I Live, Toni Braxton's, *Unbreak My Heart*, and more. Lucy checked her last yellow blinking box and paused. This was it. After this, she was the property of Ashly Martin. Her finger wavered over the button. Then she clicked, and the DocuSign flashed "completed."

That was all it took, just a few seconds to change her whole life.

She could be OK with that, she thought. Maybe she could buy a little grass shack next to her brother with the proceeds.

Only time would tell.

Chapter 4

Lucy walked back into the restaurant in a daze. Laughing, gleeful faces celebrating all around her, waitresses whisking by like little iron butterflies, sweet but efficient, trying to feed the liquored-up crowd. She took a deep breath and made her way back to the table. Her brother was already scarfing down some spider roll. The restaurant suddenly felt very stifling, full of multiple loud conversations in English and Japanese, the laughter from the tables, abrasive. If she drank a Fog Cutter full of brandy and rum that would've hit the spot, but instead she sipped some more green tea and dipped her Hamachi roll in the low-sodium soy sauce.

Had she done the right thing? She basically just sold all her songs. No one would ever hear them and think Lucy Zwick wrote these. It would be Ashly Martin's next hit. It felt like a step in the right direction, it just wasn't the fantasy she had as a little kid lying in bed dreaming of the *big time*.

"Are you OK, sis?" Neil stopped mid-chew. His big bald head reminded her of what a sweet little baby he'd been. Her little "live doll," as her mom had explained to her when he came home from St. Margaret's Hospital. Lucy had dressed him in a red stocking cap that first Christmas, making him look like a cherubic elf. How he'd never smile for anyone but her. Or that's what the adults had told

Lucy. She had liked that thought. Lucy would never have any children of her own, so he was as close to being "her kid'" as it got.

"Neil, I just sold all my songs to Ashley Martin,. she blurted, taking a big bite of some kind of shrimp dumpling.

He furrowed his brow. "*Wait*, the famous singer who dated that five-time gold medal Olympian?" Then he unbuttoned his madras shirt and pointed at the T-shirt underneath. "HER!"

"Yup." She laughed. "I didn't know you were such a big fan."

"Jenny's niece got me into her when we were back in Valparaiso, Indiana . . . for a few weeks. Her "What A Bangin Babe Wants" soundtrack was on repeat endlessly," Neil laughed rolling his eyes.

"I feel oddly . . . like I just left my kid at a bus stop and drove away. At least I'll get the songs out there. My babies will be heard." She looked over at someone setting up a karaoke machine in the bar. It seemed ironic since Ashly Martin was a sing-a-long favorite.

He smiled a wide grin. "Sounds pretty fuckin' great to me. *Cha-ching*! You didn't leave your kid at the bus stop—you dropped them off at college!"

Lucy snickered. Her brother always knew how to make her feel better. "I left Amanda a message. She should be over at Bob's right now—they're expanding the little store. Fossil Creek has become a travel destination, can you believe it?"

Neil shook his head in disbelief. "You know all those Orvis types who like to find the next hidden gem. When Dad and I used to go on our Father's Day fishing trips out east, we met a lot of them. All the Patagonia and North Face gear . . . weekend warriors. But Fossil Creek? Shit, I didn't see that comin'. It was a logger town with a bunch of ball-scratchin' tough guys. I can't believe it's so fancy pants now."

The waitress dropped the check and Neil picked it up. "Next one can be on you, when Ashly gets a platinum album."

"Haha. I don't even know if they do that anymore. I have no idea how much they're gonna pay me. It goes to the lawyer next and they hash that stuff out. Willie Nelson got quite the big gyp when he was trying to sell his songs. Hopefully Guy won't screw me."

Guy really wasn't your typical agent. For one thing, he was a little person—some people might just call him a midget—but if you met him his personality was ten feet tall. He had balls of steel and really had gone to bat for Lucy. She had hoped that his commitment was still strong.

One time another agent was trying to poach Lucy from Guy's employ and made a shitty comment about Guy: "The man is a midget, for God's sake," the scraggly agent had slurred in his Euro-trash not-quite-British accent.

Lucy had replied, "And you have big feet, what's the point, Nigel?"

"It's about image, young lady, you better get that through yer thick skull," he lashed out, looking like a trashed Iggy Pop after a hard night sleeping in the gutter.

"If I wanted my image to be a jailhouse snitch I'd have hired you."

Then out of nowhere Guy had appeared. "Are you coming, Lucy? Van's waiting outside."

And with that Guy and Lucy had flipped the bird in unison to the smirking sleazy Nigel.

Neil had a big, khaki-colored Toyota Land Cruiser—the preferred choice of tough terrain vehicles. Neil and Jenny lived in Hauula on the North Shore and mudslides were very common. Sacred Falls State Park was literally in their backyard and had been closed because many visitors had gotten hurt on the slippery rocks by the mountains and waterfalls.

Neil's retired Hawaiian neighbor Mattie had explained that the *gods* were unhappy with tourists and kids disrespecting the land and that's why accidents were occurring. From a scientific standpoint, when a downpour or hurricanes engulfed them, mud and water would pour down the mountain and the lower part of Neil's house would become a muddy river of brown water. The power washer was one of Lucy's brother's best friends. Mold had become his mortal enemy.

Lucy, like her brother, was a friend maker, sometimes reluctantly. It was ironic how they could both be entertainingly social and still gravitate toward a hermit-type reclusiveness.

Lucy's sister-in-law was in the driveway taking out the garbage when Lucy and her brother arrived back at his place for a nightcap. She had just been on a run up through Sacred Falls. Lucy's whole family was full of rule breakers, sister-in-law included.

Jenny had her braids pulled up into a ponytail. Even though she had great curls she always apologized needlessly that the humidity and her conservative job kept her from letting her hair be natural. She was Jamaican by heritage on her dad's side and her mom was Polish, but both had curly hair so it was inevitable that Jenny would be curly. She also had piercing blue eyes that could drill a hole right through you if she was pissed or just listening intently.

After she and Neil set up a couple of martinis, Jenny handed Lucy a frosty glass of iced tea with extra lemon and a star fruit for garnish. When Jenny wasn't working like a fiend she could be a great hostess. But Jenny's days at the lab were very long and Lucy's brother worked from home, so he did the majority of the house duties. Jenny's bedside reading was on immunology and his was a stack of catalogues and *Bon Appétit* magazine.

"So Neil told you for once he gets to come with on my business trip?" Jenny asked.

"Sounds pretty cool to me." Lucy nodded, taking a sip of her ice-cold refreshment.

"The place where we'll be staying is basically for people working for NASA, so I have no idea why I'm going to be working on my cancer-testing drugs there, but I'm not complaining. It's better than flying to Atlanta. Atlanta is a great city but island life is more my speed, ya know."

The CDC, or Centers for Disease Control, in Atlanta was another home base for Jenny for work. But she basically was able to use the University of Hawaii's labs for most of what she needed to do. That's what Lucy supposed, from the little info Jenny had given her. She had that military flair for keeping her lip zipped, and Lucy wasn't the intrusive type. As the years passed and Jenny was promoted, Lucy had become more curious about what exactly was with all the silence.

"What will I be doing?" Neil asked Jenny sheepishly, topping off his martini with the icy dredges from the silver shaker that had once been Grandpa's, Dad's, and now his.

"You, my dear, will be surfing, boating, skiing, or sunbathing. There's movies and restaurants. I'm sure you'll figure it out. Kelli's husband Brad is going, you like him—you guys can hang out."

Neil rolled his eyes. "Mr. Former Pro Surfer. I'd better read that William Finnegan book so I can talk gnarly waves with him."

They were sitting in Neil and Jenny's front room, which was connected to the kitchen. The last couple of years had taken its toll on the place. They had talked about selling, and getting a bigger house on the Big Island because Oahu was expensive and better deals could be found on the Big Island—Hawaii, or Hilo, to be exact—but Jenny was not able to move her lab there for some reason so they had to stay put. "I'm working on it," she told Neil when he pressed her about moving.

Neil gave Lucy his extra car so she'd have wheels while in town. The muscle car was an embarrassingly loud Sierra Gold glittering Firebird—*the Jim Rockford special*. He had bought it off some guy at the Tripler Army Medical Center who was moving from Honolulu back to Minnesota. It was earth-shatteringly loud—she was sure her neighbors at the marina were going to just *love it*. Thank God she could drive a stick shift.

They hugged goodnight and Neil shut her in his macho machine as she revved the earsplitting engine. The vibration gave her a bit of a tingly feeling.

"Now, don't get arrested, see ya on the flip side!" He chuckled.

CHAPTER 5

Lucy drove the Firebird through the hilly backcountry of Oahu's North Shore as she made her way toward the twinkling lights of Honolulu. Her iPod was playing Toto's "Africa." It seemed like the perfect smooth rock "end-of-evening" song. The traffic was nothing compared to Chicago, where she had lived throughout her twenties and into her thirties until her move to Fossil Creek. Life happens while you are busy making other plans. She could've never planned on all this!

She so wished she could call Crystal and tell her life was looking promising—maybe all those tears and fears had been worth it. How does your best friend die so suddenly? They were forty-five, they were supposed to grow into gossipy little old ladies, joking about when they were Brownies and going to the pool in their 1980s neon bathing suits. Well, now she talked to Crystal, but not on a phone.

Maybe her dad and Crystal were looking down from heaven having a couple of martinis straight up with an anchovy olive toasting her singing deal? Waikiki was where Crystal had come for her honeymoon. When Lucy's brother had moved to the island Crystal had exclaimed, "I think the next time you go to Duke's, my husband and I should meet you there for our anniversary! Won't that be fun, lounging on the beach, I'll have a margarita you can have an iced latte and we'll tell embarrassing stories that I'd rather have my kids not know until they're twenty-one!" She had laughed, taking a swig from her MADD water bottle, which was filled with Franzia box wine—she'd always been the rebel until cancer took her away.

The pier gate at the now-sleepy dock where her floating hotel room awaited her was as quiet as a wharf at midnight should be. Crickets, faraway voices, and an occasional plane overhead were the only sounds she could hear. She pulled into her allotted parking space, cut the engine of her brother's muscle car, and with a thud and a clunk she was parked. The crunch of the gravel and sand beneath her FitFlops squished with after-dark dew that seemed to settle on every surface, making it moist.

At the end of the pier she could see the little Italian white lights she had left lit on the boat so she could find her way back in the darkness. She punched a code into the security pad. It buzzed weakly but let her in.

It was kind of ironic since all you had to do was walk to the front of the white rusty locked gate, jump into the ocean, swim around the gate to the other side of the pier, and hop up to the boats. She thought about her laptop and other valuables sitting vulnerable—the latch on the boat's cabin door was not much better than a child's bike lock.

She made her way past sleeping, calmly floating yachts. A few of the arms of the pier veered out like a maze and some folks were playing music with their happy laughter echoing from boat to boat on this beautiful evening. She felt like she was in a movie and started to hum Bill Murray's "Star Wars" from his SNL comedy lounge singer skit.

This was the night she accepted a life-changing music deal in the parking lot of a sushi joint. "My life is a strange one," she said to herself. A sense of relief settled over her with each creaking step, on the old dock. This was her yellow brick road moment, here tonight in the moonlight on this weather-worn dock as she made her way to her Miami Vice–style lair.

She was getting more set in her ways as those birthdays advanced. Forty-five, almost forty-six, almost forty-seven. She had less and less desire to socialize in big groups. A few people were fine, but more than six seemed like work to her. Her partner Amanda, who had been such a recluse when they met, was now turning over a new leaf and wanted to socialize more, but on the whole they stuck with their little group. The idea of running all over the place on tours and to music festivals did not excite her, so selling her songs to Ashly, well, the more she chewed on the idea, it seemed perfect. Lucy knew she didn't have what it took to be a female rock star—the diets, the intrusions, the constant state of motion, a different town every night. In Oahu, here on this boat, it seemed so clear that chasing the musical dragon was the wrong quest for her.

Lucy made a cup of Earl Gray decaf in the mini-microwave in the galley kitchenette and went to sit topside, listening to the waves lapping against the boat, like a mother's gentle hand patting a baby to sleep.

There was something calming and therapeutic about being on the ocean—it was soothing to listen to the leaves as they rustled like grass skirts in the big overgrown palm trees that gave privacy to the marina's shore.

Many of the boats looked well worn, not all glamorous yachts as one might think. Lucy had watched a couple of broken-down-looking guys who looked like Gilligan and the Skipper bring gas cans aboard their rundown barge of a boat that afternoon.

These hermit-like bachelors were notorious old curmudgeons who docked their "wreck" toward the end of the pier, according to Jimmie Jay. "Don't talk to them, they got a screw loose," he said nervously, making the international sign for crazy with his index finger spinning around his ear.

Even in the dim moonlight she could see the guys' faintly glowing cabin light bobbing in the ocean's calm current. "They're card sharks. They both have an active card game going at the bar on a daily basis," Jimmie had added. It was their life.

Before bed Lucy called Amanda. She was snuggled into cool, fresh-smelling sheets. She had brought them from home at Jimmie Jay's suggestion. "I'm a man, I kinda stink—you should bring your own bedclothes and bathroom stuff, unless you like Old Spice," he said and then cracked up, cackling like he had just told a pee-in-your-pants-inducing joke. Despite the quick meet and greet at the marina bar when he gave her the keys, she felt a strong connection to him.

She dialed the phone and Amanda picked up on the first ring. "Hi, honey, are you having fun?" Amanda sounded so close.

"Yes," Lucy said. "It was so good to see my brother, and the boat is incredible!"

"I don't know if I would feel safe on a little boat."

Her saying this cracked Lucy up. "You shot a freaking black bear that almost killed me. A boat is nothing."

Amanda laughed. "I know the land, not the sea! By the way, Big Bob says hi." Big Bob was the owner of the local convenience/ sporting goods store and was like their guardian angel.

Amanda gossiped for a bit. It felt good to talk about normal stuff. Then Lucy told her about the music deal. Amanda was unreservedly excited, not at all wary. Lucy gave her some of the details, Guy and Ashley's people were still hashing out the exact amount she would get paid. "Lucy, whether you see it this way or not, this is a dream come true. Plus it will open doors for you tin the future. This is a miracle, *girl*!!"

"I'm so in need of less drama right now, don't think I'm nuts but I'm kinda sick of talking about Ashly Martin. Let me tell ya some more island gossip." Lucy told her someone had bought the former Magnum P.I. house. This was sad news to Lucy. She knew the TV show had been off the air for more than twenty years but to her it was a totem of good memories from her childhood. She would make her way over to see it before it was just a memory.

Lucy remembered when her dad would load up the Air Popper with Orville Redenbacher popcorn, extra butter, and sit glued to the boob tube watching Magnum and friends solve improbable mysteries while doing fantastic chase scenes around the Hawaiian islands, celebrating friendship and folly for one hour a week. Her childhood seemed to get further and further away, which was normal, but it was bittersweet.

"So what are you doing tomorrow?" Amanda asked with a yawn.

"I'm gonna lay out on the boat, take a little dip by the beach down the street, and Neil and I are going to Tuna's and maybe the **Blue Note** in Waikiki to see Kapono play. I want to hear his original songs, not just the soft rock cover songs he plays at **Duke's** at their **Beachside Brunch concert.**"

"Sounds like a plan. It's actually still really cold here—surprise—and Combover is going to the vet's bright and early." Combover, Lucy's aging English bulldog, had arthritis in his back legs and hips, only about twelve teeth left, and he farted on an hourly basis, but he couldn't be more devoted and lovable. Lucy's other pet was Tao a rescue horse who was also an old timer and he and Combover were buddies.

"I love you, honey. I'm so glad you're there, and pat yourself on the back…your music isn't dead," Amanda said reassuringly. "You know I miss you but you really needed a break from this place and all the changes you've been though. Randy and I really do have it covered."

"Thanks for holding down the fort while I'm gone. I wish you were here to see how beautiful it is on this boat at sunset."

"We will share it next year, maybe we can visit Neil for your birthday. He's a fun guy and you know I like hanging out with he and Jenny. I'll say hi to Big Bob for you."

"You do that, thanks for being so supportive. I really appreciate you having my back!" Lucy said. She hung up with a full heart.

She was ready to *conk out* so she plugged her phone in by the little built-in nightstand. It had just enough space for a phone and maybe a book under it. She breathed a deep sigh, and the silence was interrupted by someone obviously barfing into the water, not far from the window where she slept. Then she heard a plodding away into the night with the slap, slap, slap of their flip-flops.

She grinned in the darkness. This island was her second home.

Chapter 6

The glare of the morning sun woke her; she had forgotten to close the blinds the night before. Thankfully there was a small electric air conditioner above the sofa bed but it was still a bit muggy in the cabin. She got up and started the coffee—Neil would be over soon. She was happy he was coming all the way over to the boat, which was a forty-five-minute drive from his house.

She brewed her coffee and got ready for the day as she gazed out the porthole window, only to see a guy taking a not-so-secret pee off the bow of his boat. "Mahalo," she chuckled to herself.

She dressed in a light gauzy skull-and-crossbones white and gray tunic. "Gotta stay rock and roll," she said to herself, shimmying into some gray cotton crop leggings. "Love this new moisture-wicking stuff," she mused with a nod, looking into the mirror.

Neil arrived right on time to share a final cup of coffee and to check out the boat.

"This place is kick-fuckin'-ass," he said approvingly, noting some of the DVDs sitting on top of the tiny TV. "*The Beach*, with DiCaprio . . . good one . . . *Mandy*." His eyes got wide. "Don't watch this flick alone. The Carrie-lookin' chick in that movie gave me nightmares." He took a drag off his one-hitter. "Shall we motor?"

"Let's!" Lucy also took note of her brother's *island uniform*: he had a wide variety of Tommy Bahama shirts and cargo shorts, nothing too gaudy but things that always wore well in the heat. "They hide my gut and are breezy," he'd explained with a wink.

Buzz's Steakhouse in Kailua for lunch was the first stop on Neil and Lucy's hit list. There was no better way to get the retro tiki vibe of Hawaii then Buzz's. The restaurant had a great historical feel with photos of island regulars, framed matchbooks, surf flyers, antique boating paraphernalia, and cool vintage posters. It was dark and you could sit under its grass shack eaves while eating a Reuben and tossing back Mai Tais. Touristy, yes, but ironically there were not a lot of places on the island that had the old-school tiki feel.

Through the years, the Don Ho-Trader Vic's-Don the Beachcomber vibe that was so associated with Oahu and Hawaii had fallen out of favor, replaced by slicker high-end dining choices or authentic island fare, but it was undeniable that mainlanders loved the aloha 1950s kitsch. Ironically, some of the best tiki bar–type joints could be found in California and Seattle. Lucy's dad always wanted to go to Kon-Tiki Port in Chicago for special occasions. She recalled the food was about as tasty as a recooked frozen stir-fry dinner, but the atmosphere was pure Polynesian fantasy. So when Lucy gave friends places to visit on their Oahu trips she liked to think of her suggestions as, "insiders tips for outsiders."

She and her brother both left Buzz's satisfied and she picked up a T-shirt as a memento.

After lunch Neil suggested they go to the Magnum P.I. beach. "I know you're chomping at the bit to check out what's going on over there. Enjoy it now—the bulldozers are getting fired up and ready to . . . remodel, so to speak."

She and her brother watched the new version of the show, but for them nothing could replace Tom Selleck, Larry Manetti, Roger Mosley, and John Hillerman, of the original cast.

At **Waimanalo Beach**, or the *Magnum Beach*, as she liked to think of it you had to park or enter through a small concrete lot and then walk down some sandy steps and around a slightly slippery, rocky treacherous slice of volcanic stones jutting out into the ocean. Finally you would see what was left of the beach where Magnum used to toss his towel before he "dove" in for his daily morning swim. The water was actually very shallow and made a beautiful natural tidal pool that kept the area private and blocked sharks from making their way too close to swimming legs.

Neil plunked down a few foldable camp chairs and retrieved a Budweiser/Bloody Mary called a "Chelada" for himself and a bottled iced Starbucks mocha for Lucy. The sun was at peak sizzling power and they immediately felt the burn. She shellacked herself and her brother with spray suntan lotion and kicked back, taking in the wondrous view of the ocean. She could see why people came here and never wanted to leave, she thought as they passed the Pringles can back and forth, munching on salty chips from the can.

Neil popped up. "I'm gonna fish a bit," he said, polishing off his beverage and making his way into the water. Lucy was reading *The Weird World of Lagoola Gardner* by **Zach Worton**. It was a graphic novel mystery about a Hawaiian bartender. Seemed apropos. It was a fun fifteen-page read, perfect for her backpack and the beach. She'd been reading so many Hawaiian-themed novels at this point she could probably teach a class: Oahu for the Mainlander!

It was on this beach a few years earlier that Lucy had met and befriended a yoga instructor, Margo from California, and her digging dogs. One of the pooches had inadvertently tossed a crab in Lucy's crotch by accident and Lucy and Margo had had a good laugh about it. Now every time Lucy visited her brother she made it a priority to visit Margo and Tuna.

Margo's boyfriend Tuna had opened a "club" you could join—it was really a bar, but he couldn't get his liquor license, but if you paid a "suggested donation" to support the musicians you got booze and bands right out of his converted garage. Lucy explained that she had quit drinking and Margo understood since she didn't touch any kind of chemicals due to her holistic approach. Tuna had created a little menu of nonalcoholic drinks for her that other folks loved. "You can't go wrong with fresh juice and maybe a little fizzy water and agave juice on the rocks," Margo explained. "Come and try one, and stay for the nachos and the surf punk-calypso music." And with that, an enduring friendship was born. Neil had been on the island nearly fourteen years, and that's how long Lucy had known Tuna and Margo.

Tuna and Margo had really found a niche. It was one of the few places on the island where you could find tiki drinks, basic Mexican and island food *and* garage punk-surf music or calypso music, and his latest acts were some of the 1970s "Hawaiian yacht rockers" who still lived on the island and made music. The classification yacht rock was coined to give "light rock" a little more distinction. Basically it was the bridge between '70s and '80's jazzy top 40–style bands—like Little River Band, Paco, and Steely Dan—mixed with the Hawaiian flair of **Nohelani Cypriano**, **Henry Kapono (Cecilio and Kapono)**, and **Tender Leaf**. It was like Crosby, Stills, and Nash with a Hawaiian flavor. This was why she liked **Duke's** so much- she could've done without all the drunken tourists but then she would've missed seeing her fav Hawaiian troubadour, Kapono jamming out to light rock as the sun set.

Tuna and Lucy had became fast friends. He was like his own "movie of the week," as he liked to say. His dad was Samoan and mom was Japanese and they fought bitterly. He had been raised in a tenement in New York City's Hell's Kitchen. The only good thing he remembered about either one of his folks was when they would get drunk and talk about how they met in Oahu and how happy they had been. So when Tuna ran away at sixteen, he went straight to Wailea, Oahu, and got a job at the mall. Since he had no skills and was underage, the only thing he was allowed to do was "clean toilets," he explained.

Tuna had lived with four other guys in a roach-infested surf shack in the jungle where there were fights and brawling outside his door daily, usually due to drugs. His housemates ranged from old war vets to surf bums, all living together trying to keep the law away.

"But I didn't give a shit," Tuna said. "I was home and I was gonna make it work." Now he would stand by *his bar* telling *his story* with a shit-eating grin on his face, no shirt, floral board shorts, in his "slippahs" (flip-flops), knowing he had made good on his dream.

Tuna's passion included garage punk, old horror movies, calypso island music, and the light-rock stuff his mom had sung to him. He liked the song "Home" by Kapono and it got him through the scary times. "I'd lie there on my futon late at night, listening to these guys beating the shit out of each other, knowing I had nowhere else to go, so I'd put on my headphones and listen to Kapono sing about this wonderful 'home.'" He added, "I knew, I just knew I could make it if I didn't get caught up in all the bullshit." He looked kanaka—because he was kanaka, he liked to say. He was six feet five and built like a Samoan linebacker, so most crazies backed off.

After he Lucy clicked they became Facebook buddies and shared all kinds of music and comics news. She would text him stuff and keep him up on new things she found crate-digging for records on the mainland. They were loners looking for a group and they found it in their friendship. He also had a common bond with Amanda, who was big time into Harley Davidsons. He was also into "HOG's" and he rode a "Fatboy" all over the island with his Hawaiian vet brothers and sisters. So that was another strong connection that linked her to the love of Oahu.

When she and Neil were done at the Magnum beach they would probably stop over at Tuna's. Neil thought Tuna was cool. Lucy never had to twist his arm to pay Tuna a visit.

Neil was still fishing when she went to take a dip in the tidal pool, swimming out into the clear, blue glassy water to a concrete square "anchor" that was embedded in the sand below the water. Once there she paddled in place and tethered herself, kicking her legs, looking up toward the green jungle mountains and then out toward the ocean. The breeze was so soft and gentle, and she felt tears well up in her eyes. She'd been running so fast, so hard for so long . . . she just needed to stop. She had lost all her reason at some point along the way—her reason for singing, reasons for moving to Fossil Creek, Canada, and opening up a salon, reasons for getting married to Amanda . . . life had just came on fast and furious. She was just swept up in its tide. Then her dad's sad death, her brother having trouble coping with the loss. . . . What was it all about, why was she pushing so hard?

The warm water caressed her back like a kindly *tutu*-grandma in Hawaiian—and she inhaled this sacred place and exhaled all the confusion. She smiled, allowing the world to be still around her.

The tide was getting a bit higher and more folks were crowding onto their little spot. This inlet used to be so much bigger, but land erosion had carried the beach right back into the sea.

At one time she had so hoped she'd become a famous singer and buy the former Magnum cottage that sat next to the main house. That didn't look like a reality, even with Ashly Martin buying her songs.

Her brother came splashing up to her, and they both went back to shore to their seats.

"Caught not one fish," Neil said, kicking back another Budweiser Bloody Mary.

Lucy was busy drying off and beginning to pack up. She admired his art of chilling—she needed to sign up for that class! "Ready for a stop at Tuna and Margo's?" she asked. He nodded, folding up the chairs and shoving them into their little backpacks.

They rinsed off at the outdoor shower and dried off the best they could before getting back in the car.

Lucy and Neil made their way to Tuna's. It was hot as hell. Neil rolled up the windows and cranked the air. To get to Tuna's, you had to drive up a pockmarked gravel road, up a steep mountain, trying to dodge potholes and gnarled roots from the overgrown foliage that slowly enveloped you into the inner island jungle. This was not the Hawaii of postcards and sushi or brochures for the Royal Hawaiian Hotel of Waikiki; this was a lost world that Lucy felt very honored to be let into. Lucy liked to joke with Tuna, "It's because of my island Afro that I have been allowed to enter your forbidden world!"

"Sista, you know I need a haircut, you come just in time," Tuna would always respond, shaking his big bush of curls.

Finally they spotted Tuna's Place. It was like an enchanted village of multicolored twinkling lights, glass jars with fat citronella candles that sat on picnic tables. A well-equipped stage holding a sweating group of motorcycle riders playing some surf punk version of Dick Dale's "Misirlou," made Lucy kind of woozy in the heat. A cool bar made out of old soft drink machines modified to sit on their sides, stocked with ice-cold drinks to enjoy on the surfboard countertop was her destination.

Margo and Tuna lived up the way a bit farther from the actual bar, so when she was doing her yoga thing it wasn't too loud.

A cool front was coming in and a strange fog seemed to settle over the dense green forest, sneaking its way into the patio area and then suddenly vanishing as soon as it hit the light of the stage. Like smoky arms hugging you closer to the hypnotic music.

Lucy hot footed it over to the "bar" and ordered two coconut-lime rum runners, without rum in hers. They were huge and in a coconut shell you could toss into the compost pit when you were done. Margo looked so happy to see Lucy as she slid the icy drinks over to Lucy's awaiting clutches. "You're a Hawaiian hippie," Lucy teased Margo as they all sat down on one of the picnic benches.

"How do you like these guys?" Margo nodded toward the stage, looking like an island siren, fit, in her loose sleeveless tie-dyed flowing dress and long brunette curls pulled up in a loose high ponytail, touched with natural sun-kissed highlights from all her outdoor actives. Next to her, Lucy instantly felt like a pasty white Stay Puft marshmallow.

"I like this song 'Shrunken Head'!" It had funny lyrics and described a lost traveler discovering he would be the next victim if he didn't escape the clutches of a lost tribe.

"Did you just get in?"

"Yeah, yesterday." Lucy nodded.

Lucy's brother had wandered back over to the bar to talk to one of the bikers about the guy's custom Harley.

The bikers had to park their bikes up by Margo's house and be very careful coming down the hill because the back road had so much gravel and rock. If the bikers didn't go slowly, they could end up over the mountain in one wrong turn.

For some reason people just love big guys, Lucy and Margo both noticed, seeing the skinny guys crowd around Lucy's brother and the **Tongan** biker. There's a mystique. The weird thing is people also have these unrealistic expectations of how a "big guy" should be—like they should be these gladiators with no feelings. It's hard on big guys like former football players because after the limelight fades they struggle with just being a human. Neil was obviously bonding with one of the bikers, giving the "shaka" and laughing it up.

"Margo, who's that?" Lucy asked about a mountainous-looking Hawaiian guy talking to her brother.

"It's one of the MC motorcycle club guys, I don't know— could be Renegades, Pacific Knights, Wild Ones . . . I think they are doing a Cholo Ride tonight. They go to all the Mexican restaurants, I think. That's why we have a tequila special tonight, since we're one of the stops." A big gust of cool trade winds whipped through the tiki lights.

Lucy could see Neil making his way back over to them.

"Wow," Neil exclaimed, "I know his wife—she works at the **Foodland** grocery store in **Pupukea**. Last time I was in there I was buying tampons, Preparation H, Midol and Gas X. His wife, who sees me weekly, was like, 'You got problems, brah.'" They all laughed. Most stores they went into folks knew Lucy's brother because he was a six-foot-eight, bald, Will Ferrell looking—haole. He was infectiously lovable.

It was getting late, so Lucy and her brother headed back down the hill.

"You should hang out with Tuna and his wife more, they're so cool and they know everyone!" Lucy exclaimed, attempting to get comfortable in her still wet, sandy bathing suit which was riding up her rear.

Back in the car Neil opened the windows and let the breeze flow. The sun had set and it was much cooler and more comfortable but still kind of sticky.

"I'm not a socializer like you Luce…that little jaunt was more than enough for me."

"I just worry about you little brother…" Lucy said with real concern.

"You know I like my hermit life-style and Jenny gets me out…don't sweat it Sista'," he said trying to sound like a comical Hawaiian guy.

Chapter 7

Somewhere in the distance came the low rumble of a tropical thunderstorm. Lucy lay comfortably snuggled in her covers as she heard the coffeepot click on. The slow brew transformed the cabin with the earthly scent of Kona Coffee. She thought about her day ahead as she untucked herself from her cuddly cocoon.

Dressing quickly, she put her coffee into a to-go container since the boat was rocking. Already the clouds were parting and the rain had passed.

Sometimes it felt like Hawaii had a built-in sprinkler system set up by God. Just when things began to dry out a light rain would fritter in and quench the thirst of all the green things.

Neil wanted to connect downtown for brunch. "Let's meet at the **Pagoda Inn**. You are gonna love it," Neil raved.

Lucy was excited to visit "an *enchanted enclave of tranquility* right in the heart of Honolulu," which is how the review from the *Oahu Beacon* that she called up on her phone described the place.

She had some time to kill so she took a graphic novel and her coffee to the upper deck of the boat. It was going to be a lovely day, she thought as she wiped off the chair that was bolted to the platform because even a gentle breeze could knock over anything that wasn't tacked down.

The table's cup holder fit her coffee tumbler perfectly, so she didn't have to worry about it rolling off the table. The sun felt good on her skin.

Looking out at the ocean's vast expanse she had an eerie feeling of aloneness. The ocean sloshed and beckoned with its frothy waves slapping against the boat's hull, but few people were out. In this early-morning culture most people were up and out by sunrise. She was such a night owl—if she lived here she'd have to adapt.

Some luau music drifted over from another boat.—it was like an instant meditation. It was hard to get into this mind space in an urban setting. An older man in a Greek fishing cap was sitting on the neighboring boat fixing a small gadget of some sort. He nodded over and went back to his project. She could feel the manic motors of her mind instantly grind to a halt as a steel string guitar drifted over from the man's transistor radio. This was so much better than a hotel room. The world felt so placid and peaceful as she read quietly.

Thirty-odd minutes later the energy seemed to shift.

Noticing a sudden influx of people walking down the dock, Lucy checked her watch. It was time to get going. Time for breakfast!

She locked up the boat and headed down the no-longer-quiet pier. Dodging the waitresses, sailors, tourists, and workmen, she made her way to the Firebird. She rolled down the windows of the stiflingly hot car and attempted to ease her partially bare legs onto the scorching leather bucket seats. She fired up the engine. "Now we're cookin'," she said as she scared away the chickens that had been pecking lazily by her tailpipes. Chickens should be Hawaii's state bird—they were everywhere.

She got on the nearby highway and thanked God for GPS. Lucy was weaving through traffic, flexing her muscle car's V8 engine, its gold paint dazzling the other cars in downtown Honolulu. Her dad would've loved this *Rockford Files* Firebird, and she had to admit she was feeling pretty badass in this sweet ride.

After parking in the lot across the street from the restaurant, she made her way into the Pagoda Inn.

If you wanted privacy, this floating restaurant had it in magical spades. Koi ponds filled with eager fish greeted you from a maze of beautifully maintained landscaped *tranquility zones*. Little glass pagodas with private dining rooms were connected by bamboo bridges that all cross-pollinated into the main Pagoda dining room. Lucy could see a bunch of men filing out of the farthest private pagoda nearest the waterfall. She waved at her brother who was inside but still seated and he waved her in.

"Who were all those people?" she asked, confused, when a bunch of men in dark out-of-place-looking suits all nodded their good-byes.

"Business meeting. You're on vacay, I still have to work . . . sort of," he chuckled, not explaining as she took a seat across from him. He stuffed his papers into a briefcase before you could say, "Waitress." She had the feeling he didn't want her to know what he was doing.

Her dad had always joked about her elusive brother: "You know Neil, always something up his sleeve."

She had thought, "No, I don't know . . . not really." Her brother had the dominant trait of all her relatives—*NON-transparent*.

"Are you hungry, sis? Get some breakfast. I had the **Loco Moco** but they have good Eggs Benedict or Sweet Bread French toast." Loco Moco was not her bag, although the rice and gravy was kinda tasty. Every nationality has a gravy dish, and Loco Moco was the Hawaiian equivalent of biscuits and gravy, she thought. She liked it better for lunch or dinner.

Although the sun was hot, it felt cool and breezy in this hidden cove of a restaurant. There are maybe slicker, more polished places in Honolulu, but this was a unique treasure. She wished he would've brought her here sooner!

"Why haven't you ever brought me here?" Lucy asked.

"I don't know, I guess I just had so many other places to show you."

The coffee was strong enough and her French toast arrived pretty soon after.

They chatted for a bit. She could tell he felt a little guilty about leaving with Jenny for a few days. She really didn't mind, though.

"So you're sure you're OK? It's only for a few days. I just want to see what our cousins were always bragging about, plus I figured I'd better make an appearance, for Jenny's sake."

Lucy was a was a trifle jealous he was getting to go to the Kwajalein Islands. When they had been kids, her uncle from Boston had lived out on Kwaj, (as they called it for short) with their cousins and at Christmas they'd all fly back to Indiana to my Grandma's and regale us with fantastic stories of tiger sharks, scuba diving among shipwrecks, and going to school with no shoes. They were told her uncle was working on things for NASA and the Department of Defense. Now, Neil had the chance to check it out.

Jenny would be there for a month or more depending on how her research went—having connections to MIT gave her an open door to many interesting things that Lucy and Neil didn't even understand.

"You gotta tell me if it's as cool as our cousins told us it was!" Lucy said between mouthfuls of sweet French toast with homemade whipped butter and savory syrup.

He looked excited with that impish gleam in his eye. "I so will! I want to see that feeding frenzy by the docks they talk about-where the fisherman go to clean their fish and toss in the fish-guts and the sharks act like insane piranha's! "

"You better take video or I will be jealous!"
"Oh you bet I will!"

They parted with hugs and now it was Tuna time!

Tuna had texted her that he'd meet her for some "cratedigging" at Idea's used music and bookstore. Her brother wasn't really into that scene. Last time she was in Honolulu she found some great underground comics and rare vintage heavy metal Hawaiian bands on vinyl from the 1980s sporting Pacific Islander mullets to blow even Ozzy's mind. She was a music collector—it was an addiction—but it was less damaging then her former drinking habit.

Tuna was not a fan of Waikiki. Many islanders were not—it was more for tourists. "I'll make an exception for Idea's," he had texted.

Like it or not the area around her fav bookstore and music shop had completely transformed into coffeeshop row. *She liked coffeehouses.* So while she waited for Tuna she sat outside, sipping a smoky black, supremely delightful but overpriced, gourmet coffee, watching the texts roll in from work.

There had been a terrible jag of negative twenty-degree weather back in Fossil Creek. She felt kind of guilty languishing in the balmy sunshine. People were bitching because they had to go into work.

Amanda texted reassuring her. "Salon is fine, Big Bob got over there and shoveled, de-iced, and salted."

Big Bob's life had changed drastically when Fossil Creek had become a travel favorite. He'd led a pretty sleepy life running his general store and doing a bit of hunting. Last month *Montreal Life and Travel* magazine did a spread on the town with a feature about him. "They put makeup on me, Lucy," he had cried in exasperation., "I can still smell it on my beard!" He wasn't sure he liked his new notoriety. He had said under his breath, "Cuban cigar and a chainsaw, anyone?"

No snow here, she thought ruefully, sending Big Bob a selfie in the sun. He sent her back the middle finger emoji and a big smile in his coonskin cap. Lucy chuckled to herself, making the waitress give her the side eye. Lucy knew things would be OK because Randy, Amanda and Big Bob at the helm.

They had closed the university in Montreal where Amanda taught due to the freeze. "My Toyota would've made it," Amanda texted. "That FJ is a beast." Lucy and Amanda both had FJ Cruisers, which were great SUVs with one exception: they didn't make them anymore. Which was a royal bummer.

There are two kinds of folks, those who greet weather threats with a big fuck you and keep going and those who hide in the house. Lucy and Amanda were the "fuck you" types. Amanda typed, "I'm FaceTime-ing you. I'm sick of texting."

A lot of people thought Amanda was tough and gruff but she was pretty marshmallow-y when it came to certain things, Lucy being one of them.

Amanda's sweet face popped onto the screen and Lucy could hear Combover's heavy breathing. "The pup and I really miss you. This is the longest we've ever been apart, you know," Amanda said.

Amanda's FaceTime self on the phone made her look worried and sad, but also like Lucy was speaking to Amanda's inner nose. "Tilt the phone up, all I'm seeing is nose hairs," Lucy said.

Amanda adjusted the phone and Combover's bulldog-y self was right beside her, panting and attempting to lick her phone.

Suddenly Tuna appeared in a blaze of loud Harley Davidson pipe-glory, pulling up to the curb.

"Check out the ride," Lucy said with pride, pointing the phone at his new toy. He had pulled up on a cherry red CVO top-of-the-line Harley.

"Happy birthday to me!" he waved, parking the coveted high performance sports machine. Then he plunked down in the chair next to Lucy's and gave the shaka salute to Amanda.

"Heard you're having some *nice* weather there, Sista'," he called into the phone, waving at Amanda. Tuna's big longish, dark Afro was swaying in the Pacific breeze.

"For a polar bear," she responded. "Nice 'fro, bro."

"Yeah, I got my Harley hair!" He said shaking his long brown curls like a super model.

"You know I wish I was there riding with you instead of dealing with...*that*," Amanda flashed the phone at a big pile of snow she had shoveled off the porch.

He and Amanda went for a lot of chapter rides when she was in Hawaii. It was a good thing or Amanda probably wouldn't like Oahu so much. She was a Canadian through and through, though she had lived in New York City for a time; both she and Tuna were not Big Apple fans.

"OK, girls, time to break up your chitchat, Lucy and I got some *vinyl foraging* to do!" Tuna smiled wide with his big broad grin, looking every bit the Hawaiian local.

They walked across the street to Idea's bookstore, which had replaced Jelly's Hot Reads, and Lucy was surprised the store hadn't changed at all.

"Same difference, sister," Tuna said, opening the glass strip-mall door—no architectural mystique here, but the air conditioning felt good.

The smell of musty books, vinyl record albums, and the woodsy scent of the guitars for sale on the wall, with a few ukuleles that looked more like souvenirs than instruments meant for actual playing, gave the place character. Back in Chicago, the last remaining music stores were well-oiled shrines to the new revival of vinyl collectors. Lucy bought and collected it all: from cassettes to CDs to good old record albums, and yes, downloads too.

Today her focus was all "Hawaiian light rock," compilations from the '70s.

"What are you looking for?" the owner asked, perplexed. "We are out of that *Aloha Got Soul* CD."

"How about bands like that . . .ya know, local stuff."

The owner smiled his snaggletoothed grin, brushing the Malasada sugar doughnut crumbs off his aloha shirt, and guided her to the Hawaiian section. "If we got it, it's gonna be here," he said. He leaned in, his white hair brushing by her nose, like he was going to tell her a really good secret. "I'd figure out your favorite bands from that era and go look in the vinyl section. You'll probably find some real gems there." He adjusted his hat and went back up front. An hour later Tuna had an old beer box full of comics and records. He had also dug up something for Margo. "I found this Blu-ray for Margo. Deepak Chopra," he said proudly.

Lucy smiled a wide toothy grin and pointed to her box. " That's mine. Odyssey, Power Point, Aura. Do you know these bands?" she asked Tuna, looking up from her box.

"Actually, there's gonna be a reunion at **Ala Moana Hotel** with some of these bands, I hope you'll be in town to see them. I'll get the date."

They headed back over to La Marina Sailing Club to her boat.

"Oh, my God, how much you renting this for, sister? This is amazing!"

"I know! Watch your step," she warned as they stepped onto the boat's slippery deck, safely with their wares. "Jimmie Jay, the owner, hooked me up with this little stereo, so we can play our music."

Lucy brought out the little Crosley turntable, which had a CD player and cassette tape deck. "This is what he gave you? I thought you said he was into music." Tuna scoffed at the tabletop record-player unit.

Lucy explained, "His exact words were, 'I don't need no haole broad screwing up my expensive music rig on her disco shit.'" She laughed.

"He sounds like a real charmer."

"Actually, he is funny as hell. He's a retired cop, I think he bartends at **La Mariana** but I haven't seen him there. I'm doing this rental like VRBO. It was a third of the price of a crappy hotel here—you *cannot* beat this deal."

"All *Miami Vice* and shit."

"Riiiight, exactly!" Lucy thought of Crockett on his sailboat with the alligator, so outlandish, but she sure liked the fantasy of it all.

"Here, let's play my Greenwood and Manoa 3. If you like it, I'll record it for you while you're here and you can take it home!" Tuna offered.

Lucy couldn't believe her good luck, who would've thought she would have met such a perfect pal a million miles away from home and would get to listen to the "feel-good" songs of an era that was all about good times. It had only been a few days since she'd arrived on the island and already she was feeling like herself again.

Lucy made some green tea for her and gave Tuna a Phantom Bride IPA.

"For someone who don't drink you sure got good taste in booze," Tuna said, toasting her.

"I try and keep up."

They sat in the neon glow of the cramped cabin, with the windows open, going back and forth on songs and reminiscing about music and what it meant to their lives, until the sun finally set.

After Tuna left she realized how hungry she was, so she hiked up to the dock for some sashimi and poke at La Mariana's restaurant. A guy walked past her with bare feet and a trench coat, his hair burned blond by the sun as he disappeared into the bar area to collect his drink and take a seat.

She liked all the wharf-type characters who showed up here. It seemed like real locals, not just *Richie Rich types*, as she liked to call them, or tourists . . . although she was sure there were plenty of both.

The unique thing about Oahu was you couldn't always tell who had the big money. This funny guy who used to come into the Crouching Lion restaurant on the North Shore, with his captain's hat and tiny dog, looked like some daffy long-lost uncle, but the bartender had explained, "Yea, he owns half of Pupukea Point." Who knew, maybe Mr. Trench Coat was the same . . . *or maybe not.*

Lucy used to go to Crouching Lion all the time when her brother first moved to the North Shore area, also known as Deep East, the restaurant had been in a *Magnum P.I.* episode and was open later than anyplace else. The food was basic bar fare, but the view was incredible. But now it had been under construction for two years. She wondered if it would ever reopen. Maybe things were changing a little bit here in Oahu.

She really didn't know why she felt so at home here. She would sometimes find herself slipping and saying, "When I moved here," or "I love living here," but then she would catch herself.

Her brother had offered up his home in case she got sick of the boat. "I know you like a good hot bath, so feel free to hang out, watch movies, whatever. Maybe get some breakfast at Hukilau Cafe." Neil knew she couldn't resist their pancakes.

The owner of the Hukilau Cafe remembered Lucy every time she visited. "You that local musician, right, you got that big brudda' too," the owner always said.

"Musician, yes, big brother, yes, *but local,* I wish." Lucy had written a song called "Hauula" that mentioned Hukilau Cafe and the owner had not forgotten.

"I get you somma da macadamia nut pancakes," the owner offered, "'cause your CD gonna be a collector's item someday, my copy be worth a lotta money." Then she mumbled, "Your brother and his dry toast, he bother me . . . but now we friends." They both laughed.

Fossil Creek and Oahu couldn't be more different, yet they were the places she felt most at home. From this lush, vibrant, green world to the snowy hinterlands of Canada. Both suited her Gemini nature.

La Mariana Sailing Club had really stepped up its menu, she thought as she waited for her dinner.

The waitress brought her boat of sushi appetizers, and she jotted down some notes in her journal. What a great day, she sighed blissfully.

Chapter 8

The moistness is always there when you are next to the ocean or, in Lucy's case, *floating in the drink*. She had the little windows of the yacht open a bit, to catch the early-evening cross breeze. It's not like she stunk, but any little room closed up long enough gets musty, so a breeze is always refreshing.

She sat propped up in bed, feeling the boat rock and listening to the rain. It was really giving her a good roll around—the best spot was on the bed, and that was where she felt most secure.

Earlier some drunk guy had stumbled by, scaring the shit out of her, looking for Jimmie Jay. "He's out of town," she explained, realizing she could use her hot coffee as a weapon.

"Oh, OK. You all alone here?" He inquired craning his leathery neck to look around, he had the mystique of an over the hill surfer, permanently sun burnt, bespectacled and in faded board shorts…no shirt.

She replied, "You realize how creepy that sounds, don't you?"

"Oh, hahahaha." He busted out laughing. "You're are a funny girl. We got a card game going on my boat if you want to join in, we need one more person." He fixed Lucy with a steely gaze, peeling the burnt skin off his nose.

Lucy cringed as he flicked the dry skin. She also realized how cool hanging out on his yacht could be—*so very insider*—but she was tired and it was rainy and she didn't feel like socializing. So she declined.

"OK, if you wanna stop by, I got some beers and food and stuff." He patted the boat and plodded away. He was actually a pretty nice guy and if the spirit came over her maybe she'd go check out the boat folks.

There was something that oddly aged and "cured" the outdoor island people who had been on the water and outside most of their lives but were not indigenous to the "rock," as many called Hawaii. A beef jerky–style tan took over their formerly pinky skin and their hair, no matter what color it had been in a former life, now took on a bleached-out straw version, that took on the appearance of an old rope. Keith Richards came to mind.

Lucy found that her curly locks, no matter how she styled them, would go frizzy 'fro whether she liked it or not. She sighed and went back to her indoor boat activities.

A few boats pulled tarps that were tethered over their openings so they wouldn't get wet. Not all the boats docked here were meant to be lived on and yet a bad economy and sky-high housing rates forced people to get creative. Neil's former next-door neighbor was one of those people. He had been a big trader and had fallen on hard times, so he sold his house and moved onto what had been his weekend boat. He had been the first person to mention doing a "live-aboard," as a "floating hotel room," to her, but she hadn't realized it was because he was selling his beautiful vintage waterfront A-frame to make the leap himself.

She was kind of in the mood for chip and dip. So she made a bowl of dill dip with some kettle chips to munch and decided to listen to an audiobook. The rain had ceased for the moment and she contemplated sitting under the stars with her treats and listening to **David Sedaris's** *Calypso*. It was her first-ever Audible book; a friend had gifted it to her. She was excited because she was fresh from finishing *Theft by Finding*, his diary collection, and was ready for more of his oddly reassuring strangeness.

As people padded by her boat to head to the "hot card game" she wasn't going to, she sat fiddling with her phone, vainly attempting to listen to the book but only getting a sample. "Son of a bitc…" she cursed under her breath. She could not get the book on her phone to play its audio recording. Then the rain began again and that sealed the deal. She was going inside to finish her graphic novel, *The Infinite Wait* by **Julia Wertz**. Wertz's autobiographical stories were whip smart and from the heart—similar to Sedaris's, so Lucy didn't feel too cheated.

Watery waves rocked the boat, and the overcast darkness lulled her as she began to nod off while reading in the cozy lair of her bunk. The peaceful sounds of Herbie Mann playing his jazzy drifting flute, combined with her book lying on her chest, made for a trancelike quality and her eyelids became heavy.

Then *WHAM!* Something enormous slammed into the boat. She could hear chaotic voices and she raced above board to see what the hell had happened. She felt another massive *SLAM,* knocking her on her ass, swinging her, thankfully into the boat's rope rigging so she could grab it and steady herself. People were shouting, "It's got a harpoon stuck in it." Then a huge bright light coming from someone else's boat shone down on a massive shark that was dying a sad death, whacking its body between her boat and the boat right next to hers.

Some Jacques Cousteau wannabe stood on his boat and aimed something that looked like a gun at the flailing fish. The sound of compressed air hit powerfully as the impaled shark convulsed and ceased fighting, giving off a last shudder. Lucy's heart was in her throat and she didn't know whether to cry or throw up. The thing had a lot of teeth. She'd never seen a shark up that close before!

The guy was dragging the fish in and everyone was cheering. Someone playfully barked, "No night fishing, Fabian." Another person called out, "You gotta have a permit for that thing!"

"Drinks on me," yet another voice called out.

It took a lady in a fishing hat and a tube top to come over and comfort her. "You OK, honey? One of the guys said you are a guest of Jimmie's? You want to come get a drink?"

This was one of those times when not drinking booze was a real hindrance. It made Lucy look anti-social if she didn't come over for one. So she relented.

"Sure, yeah, sure," Lucy said in a daze, her heart still in panic mode.

"If you want to lock up, I'll wait," the lady said.

Lucy felt like an idiot in her *Family Guy* pajama pants and a long-sleeved T-shirt that said "I Am the Law" with a picture of Sylvester Stallone on it. The nonslip socks were a nice added touch, in a subtle vibrant orange. She put on some shoes and asked the lady if she should change, and the woman laughed. "It ain't no cocktail party over there, you'll be just fine."

The leathery drunk guy who'd invited her over earlier owned the largest yacht on the slip. So much for her presumption that he was homeless. She wasn't completely sure if he was the owner until she saw a picture of him holding a marlin hanging on the wall.

The people were all really nice, completely *not* fancy, and they made fun of her outfit but in a kind way. "*Stallone . . . and the Family Guy in one outfit?*" one guy said, shoving a beer in her hand, and smirking.

She put it on the counter and grabbed a can of Coke, "I need caffeine," she responded to the man's confused look.

It was a pretty incredible group of characters and secretly she thanked that shark for thumping its last tail slash into her boat. Hopefully there wouldn't be any damage. Everyone felt sure it would be OK.

By the time she got back to her boat she thought for sure it must have been midnight, but it was only 9:15. These island folks were early to rise and early to bed.

She was hopped up on caffeine, and visualizing that dying shark, with its bloody, impaled body and its teeth air chomping as it struggled in its last attempts to survive, was like watching a horror movie on repeat. When she tried to close her eyes the grisly vision kept running through her mind until finally she conked out, into a fitful sleep.

The night before her brother and Jenny left for the Kwajalein Islands they met at the **Canoe Club** in downtown Honolulu, where Jenny had "special access" because her boss was a member. They had **pupus** and drinks while watching the sunset. The Canoe Club had been the location for the King Kamehaha Club in the *Magnum P.I.* of the 1980s. Like a country club by the sea.

Tiki torches were lit, the stars blinked bright in the night sky, and Lucy was on her second nonalcoholic beer of the night. Her sister-in-law had her braids up in a ponytail and looked like a tiki goddess with her cocoa-colored skin, in her black and red aloha-patterned dress cinched at the waist, and sporting a pair of strappy black high heels. Neil was wearing his usual Tommy Bahama silk blend guayabera shirt distinctive for its front embroidery. This one was covered in little tiki masks and palm fronds. The colors were understated, so he didn't look too garish. The fabrics were what gave away whether you were a tourist or a local. Polyester/cotton/spandex blends didn't do quite as well on a steamy night as the cotton, chambray, silk blends. Lucy's ensemble was a quirky version of a Mexican peasant dress. The dress was long and cool, flowing down to her ankles, with tiny sugar skulls crocheted around the bust. Her trusty sparkly FitFlops added some comfortable razzle-dazzle.

"Only you could find that dress with the cool skulls," Jenny complimented Lucy in mock shock.

"I used to have one with black cats woven into lace covering the back of this same type of dress. My friend who made them called the collection her Stevie Nicks–inspired Witchy Woman Collection."

"Does she still make them?

"She disappeared . . . like, literally. I went to her shop with a friend. I pull up to her store and it's a guitar repair place? I go inside and the guy tells me he's subletting from her while she's in Europe. He even had a jacket of mine that she had been mending!"

"So did she come back?"

"Nope, I've never seen her again. I even went to the Renegade Craft Fair, a couple years later, where I had originally met her. People remembered her, but no Renee."

Lucy shared the shark story with them and even the waiter was all ears. "Yeah, it's sad. This climate change has warmed up the waters and so they have come in closer to land, more shark attacks and shark sightings than usual, for sure," Jenny explained.

She took a sip of her vodka tonic and added, "They've seen a lot of hammerheads off the Kwaj, too. One of my co-workers took video of three sharks that got stuck in a semi-shallow area. Very, very strange. They're not social—they're reclusive creatures."

She explained that most of the time she was in Kwaj she would be at the Lincoln Laboratory. "The island used to be more focused on weapons and ballistics but my focus is closer to medicines lurking right on the sea floor. . . ." She trailed off, closing the topic down.

The wind was strong, and the tiki torches whipped and danced around on their fat wicks, with the strong scent of citronella was pungent. "The wind is what's really repelling the bugs," Neil explained.

Food was served. While they were enjoying their meals, Jenny interjected, "Neil is going to have a *buddy* on the island." Jenny smirked, patting Neil's shoulder.

He rolled his eyes. "Don't make me not want to go," he sighed. "So, Jenny's lab partner's husband Stew"—Neil dragged his name out in a long *ewwwww*—"is really into talking, and I do repeat talking, mostly about surfing." Neil took a swig of his beer and continued. "I've never seen the guy surf, he just talks about it endlessly. He is also a real estate agent for East Oahu Realty and he can talk *endlessly* about the homes, the market . . . blah, blah, blah . . . he used to work for some other company who sold Gwyneth Paltrow a house here. It's all I heard about for days, every conversation steered back to *Gwyneth*."

Jenny jumped in, "In case you were confused, Neil's not a big fan."

Neil continued, "I remember, just to see if he was listening I would reply back to him in Welsh. I only knew like three phrases— it's a long story. I'd say, '*Iawn, Diolch,*' which is 'OK, thanks,' or '*Beth wit ti'n wneud,*' '*What are you doing,*' and the bastard would just keep talking. I could've said, I shit in your soup and he would've nodded and replied, 'Great, great.'"

This was a side of Lucy's brother she adored—his weirdo side! "My question is, why were you trying to learn Welsh?"

He got an impish, childlike look on his face, "I really love Super Furry Animals, that band," he said, "and the lead singer had just put out an all-Welsh album, so I mistakenly thought I could learn it—ya know, 'cause I'm so good with languages, NOT!" He rolled his eyes and flicked his own forehead.

"You are my brother," Lucy reached over and gave him a quick hug. "I own Mwng, I love that Gruff Rhys singer, don't understand a word of it but it's got the grooves!"

Jenny was staring at them like she'd just smelled a rotting raccoon. " The DNA is strong."

They were all saved when Jenny introduced them to some people who stopped by the table.

Jenny obviously was something special because the *men* who came to the table also looked pretty impressive with their wives in tow. Jenny and her lab partner were the only females on the "project," it seemed.

After dinner, they dropped Lucy off at her boat. It was only 8 p.m. "Another late one," Neil commented, but he was serious. "Lights out by 9:30 in our house." He winked.

Lucy could tell Jenny wanted to check out the boat but he was antsy to get home.

"I'll be here when you guys get back, you can come over then," Lucy offered.

The whole wharf was alive on a Friday night but she was ready for some green tea and a good book.

Chapter 9

The first thing that was honking him off was a four-hour flight with no movies. *They were sorry but there was a problem.* He was not a reader but he was going to read something since he and Jenny were not sitting next to each other due to an overbooking in Economy and she had been sweet enough to give his big six-foot-eight ass the first-class ticket.

He was settling into the big leather La-Z-Boy–style seat, fumbling for his old scratched-up iPod, when the lady next to him asked, "How tall are you, young man?"

A pinch-faced colonel's wife who seemed way too talkative was his seatmate. Oh goody, goody, he thought, his annoyance palpable. He didn't want to piss her off because who knows, he could be having dinner with her tonight. Kwaj was a small island, very small.

"You know what they say about boys with big feet?"

His face suddenly felt flushed and pink, Jeeesus, this old bat was getting frisky with him. He just laughed, and hailed the steward, ordering an extra strong bloody, "Ya know, make it two, I'm a big boy," he smirked at the lady, who was now giving him big wide eyes. She reminded him of one of the country club ladies he'd grown up with, very toned and tan, with her short patchwork golfing skirt tight to her thighs and a pink Ralph Lauren polo top, with still-perky tits.

She was stroking her arms and finally put on a little yellow sweater. There were some nice rocks on those bony fingers. "So how long you been married?"

She snorted, "Long enough." She rolled her clear blue eyes and took a sip of her whiskey sour. "Thirty years."

"Me, the wife back there," he said, thumbing to the midsection of the plane. "We've been together since high school almost, now married eleven years."

She snorted, "Good luck keeping the flames alive, you boys get bored *real* quick." She cocked her head sideways, now checking out the boy candy that was their very tan flight attendant who had been giving Neil the big eye since he'd boarded.

This plane felt like a pickup bar and he wasn't in the mood.

She finally realized it wasn't going to happen and cracked open a romance novel with a Fabio-looking guy on the cover in a lusty embrace with a scantily clad maven. Those books were a setup for the failure of romance reality.

He closed his eyes, letting Neil Young's *Harvest Moon* soothe him into a fitful snooze.

He knew he was dreaming but it felt good, little warm licks on his toes, ummm, yesss- he was snuggling into the ticklish goodness. Until a jarring screech, and a dog's yelp shocked him awake. "Biffy," the colonel's wife said, nervously jamming her little Maltese dog back into its soft crate that had come undone under his seat. The mutt had been licking his toes and now warm urine was on his flip-flop from the abrupt bouncy, landing.

"Welcome to the Kwajalein Islands, you can now unbuckle your seat belts, have a safe trip!" the uniformed host announced, savoring his big curtain call.

As Neil cleared out the overhead bin he noted the horny granny slipping the steward her phone number as she slipped off the plane with her dripping dog carrier.

He had a feeling this trip was going to be anything but the usual inner-island jaunt.

Chapter 10

She was learning quickly how important the weather was when you lived in a boat. Tube Top Lady explained some of the boat owners had "micro-apartments" on land so they could bath, do laundry and escape in case of a hurricane.

The ocean at night can be scary. It crashes, bashes, and drives itself full throttle right into shore . . . and it's loud. The "wave breaks" that call out in the inky darkness must be monstrous—it literally sounds like the ocean is bulldozing itself to shore. Until the placid waves of morning arrive.

They say the summer waves build sand onshore and higher winter waves move sand offshore, but Oahu's beaches are shrinking and sometimes at night when Lucy stayed with her brother so close to shore, where the waves were practically tickling her bedroom windows, she would get nervous. So imagine these same waves licking the boat like a hungry mauling bear, pawing and pushing its stern and bow like a circus toy.

She lay in bed, feeling vey small. The darkness all still around her at 2 a.m., she realized she had a long night ahead of her. Maybe she should've checked out the weather. She had actually taken some seasickness pills. Sooner or later the morning would save her.

To calm her mind, she listened to *Calypso*, David Sedaris's audiobook. It was *finally loaded* up on her phone and she was eager to listen and drown out her fears. This boat was tethered so tightly to the dock it was practically glued to the dock. Twenty feet away were mangrove-type foliage cushioning the shore, and other, bigger boats also lashed tightly to the docks seemed to take the wind for her. She wondered if she would ever do this type of rental again.

The boat tossed and vibrated as David talked about living in Sussex, England. They got their share of rain and weather there but he wasn't on a boat. It sounded so safe and grounded.

His topic veered to aging. Getting old, the indignities he was speaking of, she was just starting to comprehend.

Watching Jimmie Jay's thumbtacked paperwork schedules flutter to the floor exposing a Dita Von Tease calendar still hanging on his cork board wall by the kitchen sink. The constant vibration of the boat made it look like Dita was gyrating in her sexy getup. Lucy still enjoyed dressing up but now it wasn't in binding clothes…she preferred rock and roll t-shirt, black leggings boots and jackets. Not very Hawaain but perfect for Canada or Chicago.

The boat was beginning to calm down. She just had to ride out the storm the best she knew how. Great metaphor for life, she chuckled.

She had done a little meditating that morning and it had occurred to her that island living felt much more sane. On the mainland life came fast and furious, it was people, honking cars, barking dogs, fast cars, loud music—things were high energy, high anxiety; blinking lights, all-night, twenty-four-hour businesses. You had to make a concerted effort to find calm.

When she drove around Honolulu after dark, a certain "closing up of the shutters" seemed to occur. It seemed more natural to her. But, she mused, she was on vacation. Maybe it would be different if she was here working.

The morning did come, peaceful as a sailing bird on the wind. The dock was active with people who didn't seem to be as worked up about last night as she was. "You at least removed the windage, so stuff wasn't blowing right into the drink." The Tube Top Lady, who'd invited her over the other night, commended her.

These people and their chat reminded her of a close-knit subdivision, like a nautical "Knots Landing"—she snickered while listening to neighbors complain about who didn't pay their slip fees, who was shagging who and the boat's that were complete pigsty's…the general neighborly feuding and cliquishness that goes on in a mainland cul-de-sac. She liked being the voyeur!

Lucy decided today would be a relaxing beach day and she'd head over to **Turtle Bay** for some sun. It looked a bit overcast and windy but usually that would transform into a sunny, island dream by the time she got to her destination. That was the beauty of Hawaii: a certain kind of predictability.

She packed a turkey sandwich and some mango chunks into a couple of Ziplock bags and tossed in some kettle chips, she filled her canteen with ice water, and she was ready to go. She had already packed her beach bag with her swimming shoes, *Mojo music magazine*, her ever present journal and **Jessica Hopper** music critique book. Sunscreen spray 30 and 50, Shesido 47 sunblock for her face, her red bucket hat with golden skulls embroidered all over it—*because why not?*—and two extra thick beach towels. Oh, and her ever-present iPod. She would freak out if someone stole it since they didn't make them anymore and she wanted her music available since *streaming* on the island was spotty.

Tuna texted her that there was a good band at Haleiwa Joe's in Kaneohe and would she like to meet them around 7:30 or 8. She texted back, "HELL YEAH!" Her day was planned! This was shaping up to be the perfect vacation!

She and Amanda talked all the way to Turtle Bay via Bluetooth—when technology worked it was a beautiful thing. Fossil Creek was getting another round of snowstorms, so Todd was watching the horse and the dog and Amanda was staying in

Montreal at her friend Renee's so it would be easy for her to get to the class since she was teaching a course at **McGill University**.

The roads from Fossil Creek to Montreal were just too dangerous. Todd, her band's lead guitarist, was always happy to house-sit. Since Lucy and Amanda had just installed a hot tub and she could imagine he would be sipping a Jack and Coke with the jets on high.

Lucy parked right next to a state or the art lizard green luxury Lamborghini **Urus**…which looked like Uranus at first glance…That was too much "fancy stuff" for her she lamented peeking in the window and not even knowing exactly where the radio was located. She'd take her brothers "bygone era of feathered hair, one-night stands, and disco balls any day. She took her beach stuff out of the back seat. Her backpack waterproof backpack being full of food, towels and entertainment made her giddy.

Tiptoeing through the now hot sand she scanned the beach full of out of towners for a good spot. It may have been touristy but it was a lovely spread.

She plunked down her stuff at a distance from the little kids romping around, finding a nice secluded spot off to the side. She had just gotten settled when she realized the guy behind her was giving her a bit of the stink eye. Maybe he felt she should've moved farther from him.

Calm down, Mr. Entitlement, she sighed, trying to settle in. Just as she leaned back and let the sun blowtorch her cadaver-like whiteness, she realized who the guy was—*Jack Knivves*, the famous adventure novelist!

Great, here she was in all her flabby whiteness, a few feet away from one of her favorite authors. She wanted to tell him about the song she wrote for him, "The Sun Never Sets (On Jack Knivves)." Her heart and gut were a flurry in nerves. Then she realized she should say nothing. She had sent him the song, he'd never responded, he was a notorious prude and recluse. She shook her head, "chill out" she said to herself, and decided to read her Jessica Hopper book.

The sun was bearing down on her and she couldn't seem to get comfortable. Ugh!! She could not concentrate. She couldn't stop thinking about Jack Knivves. If he walked by, she could say, "I'm a big fan." Yeah, that seemed like a plan.

When she finally had the nerve to turn around, he was gone. Part of her was relieved but this was indicative of her life and not being able to schmooze, she was always leading with the chin.

Then it occurred to her she was selling her songs to a Grammy-winning singer without doing any ass-kissing. So, she should just be thankful and stop judging herself.

Rolling onto her back, she propped her head on the rolled towel, plugging her earphones in and putting on the Beach Mix. The first song was "Solar Sex Panel," a strange song that was a minor hit by **Little Village**, but actually it was John Hiatt, Ry Cooter, and Nick Lowe singing the most surprising uplifting song. It was the perfect feel-good song for this beautiful day.

She plunking her bucket hat over her face. It was nap time!

She must have dozed off for a half hour or so because the sun was really searing down on her when she awoke. It was time for a dip! She walked down to the water and put her toes in the surf. The white bubbling waves felt like fizzy Alka-Seltzer tickling her feet. It wasn't too cold and she slowly made her way into the water, trying not to think of sharks or other sea creatures. She felt safer being on this populated beach, with a natural wide rock formation in the center of the bay like a "safety" swim area. A man with his dog was taking kids back and forth on his surfboard, hour after hour, she had seen him here many times and it was reassuring.

As she paddled around the gentle waves she wondered if her brother was having a good time. It would have been so cool to be on the Kwaj, she had heard so many vivid stories about it growing up. Those tales had sparked her imagination for island living.

One of her cousins had been stranded on a floating swim platform off shore sunning herself when the lifeguard started yelling, "Tiger shark, don't go into the water," and she was so terrified of being stranded she supposedly jumped in the water and swam to shore. Real or fake story…Lucy would never know.

Her other cousins would brag about how they could wear their swimsuits and shorts to class with no shoes.

Diving off old ships that had sunk halfway into the water and were now like little private islands were one of her cousins' after-school pastimes. Supposedly, these oxidizing wrecks were all over the surrounding shoreline, and cousin Claudia had cut her foot open diving off one of them. She had explained, "We all meet up on the boats, we're not supposed to." The half-sunken husks sounded mysterious and forbidden to Lucy, a kid from northwest Indiana. It all seemed so exotic!

Neil was probably meeting all these cool James Bond–type people. She wished she could've gone but she was enjoying her own special trip and he'd be home soon enough.

Chapter 11

They had just put in a new pool on the grounds where Neil and Jenny would be staying—"That's the good news," their host Barbara DeKroner explained, with her ever-so-delightful swinging ponytail and surf-ready body, full of positive energy and cheerfulness.

Then she unlocked the door to Neil and Jenny's room, trying to soften the blow with the promise of unlimited booze—"And we are having a tequila tasting in an hour!" Neil now understood why they were heaping special food passes and entertainment amenities on them. "Unfortunately, we had to relocate you to our more vintage barracks due to the last storm, which wiped out the progress on the new building you were supposed to stay in." She smiled, looking efficient.

"I'll be working," Jenny explained, "so I won't be in the room much. I'm sure Mr. Zwick, my husband, will be busy snorkeling in the lagoon, sailing, or taking a ham radio class I signed him up for." Neil wasn't listening, he was too busy being in shock by his surroundings.

It was the lovely scent of mildew that greeted his nostrils first. Neil noticed the squishy feel of the indoor-outdoor gray carpet that matched the stark cement industrial cinderblock gray-painted walls.

If he was into kitsch, the 1968 polyester floral bedspread, with more than a few cigarette burns melted into the fabric, would have been more interesting. The bright yellow-painted faux bamboo tables next to the bed that should have retired to a Florida garage sale back in 1976 had somehow made it all the way to Micronesia! *This did not look like the brochure!*

The bed was only a full size, so his six-foot-eight body would be drooping off this glorified cot. The pièce de résistance was the large faded art over the gray metal aluminum Steelcase office desk, hung slightly askew for effect, —this "Debbie Downer" with dreary dying cornfields and a distant somber farmhouse was a misery-inspiring piece called *Autumn Cornfield* by Andrew Wyeth.

Neil sighed, shaking his head, as he heard the hotel room door discreetly click shut as Barbara made her hasty exit. This room could make a person forget hope ever existed. The giant cane spider lying belly up in the crusty corner of the room was a nice touch, too. At least it was dead.

He and Jenny propped up their suitcases on the metal desk. He sure as shit didn't want the fabric of their suitcases touching the floor of this petri dish, who knew what microscopic creatures lurked in the mushy fibers of this carpet. They both changed carefully Jenny leaving for the lab and Neil headed down to the pool.

"Tequila time, motherfucker!" Stew ran up to greet Neil, in his black and white checkerboard "swim trunks". "Check them out, Van's man, pretty bitchin'!"

"*Yes, bitchin'.*" Neil agreed sarcastically. Did Stew think he was Spicoli…He needed a very large drink, stat.

Neil hotfooted it to the table by the DJ, hoping to drown out Stew's chatter, with copious amounts of top-shelf tequila. Clase Azul, in its beautiful white and blue ceramic bottle, sat beckoning his taste buds, as the ripe limes sat juicy in iced bowls along the bar's display. DeLeón looked more like an expensive perfume then an elixir from the agave plant. Neil was shocked they even had Gran Patrón Piedra on the menu, this was after all a government-sponsored event, they usually didn't go this pricey. "Two ninety-six a bottle but at the PX we can give you a far better deal if you are interested," the bartender explained.

Neil ordered a Casa Dragones—this was not a tequila made for a margarita. He would savor this as the sun set.

Then Stew's voice crashed into his moment of tasting bliss. "I found this website for the best board shorts, seriously. It's called Farfetch and it's fuckin DOPE! Hurley, *get the fuck out.* I'm talking Fendi, O'Neill, Timo with the tiger print."

Neil realized he could've completely ignored Stew and Stew would've just kept talking, and that's just what he did . . . and that's just what happened.

". . . and the seven-inch board short, not too long, not too short, are my best bet in length," he blathered on while attending to his expensive French crop haircut, styled forward to give him that boyish edge. "In my profession I always have to look ready to impress, so I bought the Dolce & Gabbanas but they got stolen, Versace pinch my waist, I mean I'm actually surfin' in these bad boys, ya know. Wait till you see my Orlebar Brown with the Monte Carlo print, you are gonna want a pair."

Oh, my God, help me, Neil's mind cried out, over and over. He forgot that no amount of booze could make Stew palatable. He knew there was a "dock excursion" where you could watch as all the fishermen who came into port cleaned their fish, then they dumped the guts into the bay, which created a shark feeding frenzy, he'd promised his sister he'd take pictures. One little slip and Stew could live up to his name—Stew could be an actual stew for hungry ocean "fishes."

Neil couldn't decide if he should ask Stew about his job so he would stop being a human clothing catalogue or just keep letting him talk, and go jump in the pool.

He decided to jump in the pool. It was a saltwater pool, but beautiful. He did a few laps and as the warm sun loosened up his spirits, he realized he needed to stop his personal pity party. This was his wife's big chance to really move ahead at her job, he was in a pool, drinking booze in the middle of the afternoon—Jesus, what more could he want? Well, a little weed would be pleasant but he'd survive.

Suddenly his head thunked into a human body. "Whoops, I must've jumped into your lane," a familiar voice coyly chuckled.

He flipped over from his backstroke to apologize, only to stare into the eyes of none other then . . . THE COLONEL'S WIFE! No, no, no—not the lady from the plane!

"Remember me from the plane?" she gushed. She wore a vintage flowered swim cap that crowned her head like she was in a 1940s Esther Williams movie doing an "aquacade" impression.

He scratched his neck, which felt hot and itchy. He nodded and tried to smile. "Don't you love the new quarters, I actually feel like I'm on vacation for a change instead of in municipal public housing." She was giggling like a schoolgirl. She obviously was in the "new" section, he thought wryly.

Neil looked at Stew waving from the beach table pretending to strangle the umbrella's neck, then he weakly smiled back at the Colonel's Wife. What had he done to be mired in this fresh hell?

"That man is drunk, he should be cut off," the Colonel's Wife said in disgust. Neil realized who she reminded him of: Mrs. Smails from *Caddyshack*. If he didn't stop this cavorting, he'd be stuck "loofahing her stretch marks," he thought with a slight chuckle.

"He's Norah's husband, better go check on him," Neil said, as if that explained everything, as he quickly swam away from Mrs. Smails.

Making his way back to the bar, he realized maybe it was time for a bike ride. The bartender poured him a healthy shot of Tres Agaves, Neil took a pull off the lime, downed the shot, and made a break for freedom, rushing past a confused Stew, calling out, "I left something back at the room!"

Neil quickly strode past the kiddie pool. Freedom was just in sight, but one last reminder of reality came as stepped full force on a rock-hard plastic, teeny-tiny LOL Lego doll. His now-throbbing bare foot a reminder he should put on his flip-flops, he tossed the little toe breaker back into the pool while swearing under his breath. He felt a certain exhilaration from his escape.

He could see the bike rack with bikes you could rent by the hour. He popped in a few of his tokens from Barbara, and suddenly he felt free. He heard someone blasting Def Leppard's "Rock of Ages," and it seemed like his breakaway anthem: *"Rise up, gather round, rock this place to the ground, burn it up, let's go for broke, watch the night go up in smoke! No serenade, no fire brigade—just a pyromania!"*

He took a deep breath, letting the island air floating off the salty ocean fill his lungs. When was the last time he'd ridden a bike? He passed tidy blacktopped streets. He kept to the one main street, past B.Q. (Bachelor Quarters) apartments and other housing, a Surfway Grocery, and a park with an outdoor movie screen, all these sights he took in as he headed toward the beach.

Kwaj Lodge, where he'd be tomorrow night for some cocktail party event, looked pretty cool. As he passed some kids at a skate park, he noted the nice big scar on his knee from the last time he'd attempted to skateboard. It was a young man's sport for sure, he reminded himself.

If he could describe this main thoroughfare in one phrase it would be "A Very Brady-Looking Village," as in the television show *The Brady Bunch*. This island area was midcentury modern all the way, with the low ranch-style concrete buildings, the minimalism design, tiki kinda stuff here and there, very clean lines, and well-manicured foliage for a totally tropical island from the era of Gilligan.

He recalled the map he'd looked at on the plane ride over and knew there was some place called the Surf Shack. He should be getting close. He spotted some young, athletic-looking kids in swimsuits, with wet hair and towels around their shoulders kidding around and figured he must be getting close.

Sure enough he followed the signs and before he knew it, it was beach time. Parking the bike, he felt odd not locking it up, his old Chicago ways making him leery of leaving a bike just parked in a rack.

There was a drink area that looked like a tiki bar and he actually just ordered a Dr. Pepper. He could use the caffeine and sugar, he thought.

There were still a few more hours until sunset and he sat down by the rocks. In the distance a partially submerged World War II sea vessel, a rusty relic to a sketchy past, was being used as a diving platform. A few people were climbing on board to the jagged hunk of metal and jumping off. He must be getting old—to him it just looked dangerous.

He couldn't help thinking that the largest shark sanctuary in the world supposedly was somewhere around here. How could he swim here? One of Jenny's friends who lived out here for months at a time would go diving at **Coral Head**: "Dude, it's like a shark party going on, I got some great shots with my GoPro." People snorkeled with the sharks like it was no big deal, but he was just not that brave. He was really *jonesing* for some smoke. There was no fuckin' way he'd find weed on this island or even ask for it—military employees and soldiers could lose their jobs for smoking pot. He was a wake-and-bake kind of guy, so this put a crimp in his routine, but it was only three days.

His mind started to wander as he relaxed. He felt bad leaving his sister back on Oahu but she was easily self-entertained. He figured, let her go to Duke's and hear that guy she liked sing, and do her arty-farty things.

When he returned he and Lucy had plans to hit **Turtle Bay Beach** and **Lei's Lei's** for some sunset nachos, then he'd take her to **Waikiki Aquarium** to see the jellyfish, the **Polynesian Cultural Center** for some souvenirs, and maybe a little horseback riding at **Kualoa.** Who knows what else, she was pretty easygoing. He'd get to fill her in on Kwaj, too.

Neil couldn't figure out why Lucy wasn't more excited about this pop singer who was gonna record her songs. He would have exploded with joy if he got a paycheck like that, but he didn't get "artistic integrity" and all that shit. Money talks and bullshit is just bullshit, but this was real. He wouldn't mind having his sister as a neighbor! He decided he would talk her into the deal, if he could.

"Hey, mister."
Neil looked around, there wasn't a soul around except for some kid. "Me?" he replied.

"Yes, you." The kid gave him the side-eye as if to say, no shit, who else would I be talkin' to? "You like boat rides?"

He began making excuses, he could tell this kid was selling something, "I'm good, ya know. . . ."

Before Neil could finish his sentence the kid whispered, "You like to smoke?"

This stopped Neil in his tracks. "Maybe, why?"

"Maybe I got a Wacky Weed boat cruise leaving tomorrow at 9 a.m."

Neil pondered this invitation for a moment. "I have to be back before five, I have to attend an event."

The kid looked smart and on the up and up. Neil should know, he'd dealt with enough lowlifes in his career of herbal entertainment.

"Oh, yes sure. We should be back around three. You smoke, eat nice food, I take you to little island for swim and we come back by three, no problem."

This young buck was the answer to Neil's Stew and Mrs. Smails problem. He did a silent prayer of thanks.

"I'll be here at nine sharp," the kid promised, as he stood very straight and succeeded at looking very professional, in his blue aloha shirt and pressed khaki shorts. "Please do not forget to bring sunblock we will be on the ocean all day, a hat and a towel are recommended, and appropriate boating footwear, like what I am wearing." He pointed to his lace-up water shoes, which looked like they could hold a grip on a boat pretty good. The kid had a nice presentation.

"Oh, yes, how much is this little excursion gonna cost me?"

The kid looked suddenly nervous, like he hadn't thought about a price. "Um, because of food and ya know . . . well, the package rate is $100."

Neil felt pretty good about that price. The guy was no cop, that was for sure. Still, he let the kid sweat for a minute.

The boy stood taller and added, "Ice cold beer, too." The young entrepreneur sweetened the pot.

"I'm in."

The kid looked excited and showed him where the boat was docked. "See you at nine."

Neil used his very powerful visual skills, imagining a day without Stew or Mrs. Smails asking to rub lotion on her wrinkles. The choice was clear: an unauthorized, possibly illegal boat tour was the only choice for him.

Chapter 12

A day at Turtle Bay's lovely beach had make her grimy with spray sunscreen, she kept shellacing herself every time she got out of the water to avoid lobster status and now the sand and salt felt like a waxy second skin.

She was close to her brother's house and she had the keys- he had invited her to come over while they were gone so…might as well freshen up there and then maybe get a "fried chicken plate lunch" for dinner at Keneke's which was close by.

As she drove along Kam Hwy she scanned for his hidden driveway. He was becoming more and more hermit-like in his "old" age. His place was seriously tucked away but there was a lava rock with two diamond reflectors right at the mouth of the entryway, that alerted you to his driveway. The opening was super crowded with lush green vegetation to keep it private but as soon as you turned into the gravel driveway, you were presented to a breathtaking house on the ocean.

She found the turnoff and pulled in. Motion sensor lights illuminated a majestic home on stilts. There was a seawall in the distance, beyond the house. Here a long neglected swing hung from a gigantic weeping tree that gave shade to the home mid-day when the sun was hot.

The one neighbor to the left was a sweet but nosy TuTu (grandma in Hawaiian), that Lucy had enjoyed a few conversations with, then to the right was an adorable vacant house, that was quickly falling into disrepair. She always thought of how cool it would be to rehab this mid-century fixer-upper with it's still intact sliding glass doors that faced the Pacific Ocean. When the old lady who lived in it died the powers that be let it rot until the "lease" on the land was up and then it would be sold. It was such a cool relic from the modernist movement, she couldn't believe with all the glass and teak wood that it had survived since 1965 it was like a "*Mad Men's* vacation hideaway" and it made her sick to see it vacant when someone could be raising their family or vacationing there.

From her car she had to deactivate the alarm from her phone- it was a very intricate system. As soon as she was in the house it would reactivate on its own unless you cancelled it. Anything over 50lbs. would set it off, if walking on the property. "Jesus Neil, got some enemies," she had joked.

He had shrugged.

She cancelled *all* the alarms and made her way up the outside stairs noting all the beautiful plants Neil and Jenny cultivated. So much love had gone into the house. She unlocked the red front door and went in. There were a few more stairs up to the landing, until the first floor. You better not break a leg or it would be a real pain in the ass, she thought as she tossed her beach bag by the front door landing. She didn't want to drag in any leftover sand on their beautiful dark wood floors. She recognized the overstuffed leather couch they had bought years ago at Marshall Fields in Chicago- it had withstood multiple moves and still looked great. She opened the screen doors that faced the ocean and a whoosh of air immediately refreshed the stuffy room.

The guest bathroom off the hallway was perfect and had a deep soaking tub of which according to her brother was "a big waste of money" because no one ever used it. She would be happy to take advantage of its 6 jets and light a little candle on the sink for mood! She would rinse off downstairs first, but she wanted to grab his big Hugh Heffner robe. It was obnoxious and playboy-ish, with a royal purple terry and gold piping and his initials on the front pocket.

She grabbed it off the hook on the back of the bathroom door and scurried back outside to the rinsing station and tried to get off all the beach mung from her bod. It felt a little eerie to be out here alone. The sun had set and besides the scant security lights under the house where she was scrubbing off…it was pitch back and quiet. You could barely find this place in the light let alone the dark, so she felt pretty safe.

She dried and peeled off her suit quickly putting on the robe. There was a hook for the suit to drip dry and now for some bubbles!

Padding back up to the house her flip flops made a squishy sound, she just hoped not too much sand had followed her.

She made an aloe-water and soda mocktail and filled it with ice. Flipping on some Crosby, Stills and Nash on the stereo she began to fill the tub. She added some tropical smelling bath salt and slid into the steamy water. She felt a slight sting where she had missed the SPF on her shoulder and had a bit of a sunburn, but other than that she felt a bit woozy and peaceful.

She closed her eyes and the song "Wasted On The Way," lulled her into relaxation mode.

Without warning a crashing BANG, BANG, BANG came from the front door. It was such a jolt her heart leapt, and for a moment she was breathless… she threw on her robe, looking helplessly around the bathroom for some kind of weapon. She grabbed a crusty looking toilet plunger, then she ran as stealthy to the kitchen, also taking a very expensive looking butcher knife from its block, she padded back down the hall to look out the little side window.

"Neil godammit, I'm racing for time. I know you're in there… open the goddamned door!"

There was a guy in a bubble gum pink polo shirt and matching pink pants in a pair of Gucci loafers, his car that looked like…*a silver DeLorean*, it was still running, and loudly, at that.

"I can see your car Neil!" He bellowed.

Lucy thought, if he was a killer she could distract him with the dirty toilet plunger and then stab him with the gigantic knife.

She tightened her robe straps and went down to open the door.

The well groomed but sweaty man was obviously shocked, then a look of knowing crossed his eyes, "Oh, shit…I forgot Neil's out of town you must be his sister."

"And you might be," she answered nervously.

"Oh crap, yea…I'm the guy from the yellow house down the street-Neil and I are tight. Listen, this is serious business," he retrieved a mesh bag from his pocket, "I need you to give this to your brother. Please do not tell a soul, I have no choice but to hope you are as trust worthy as your brother. Give him this, he will understand when he gets back."

Almost throwing the bag at Lucy, he hugged her tight, "this is my life, ok," he nodded desperately.

"I understand," Lucy responded. "Uhm sir," she called out as he was turning to leave, she mimed, *wipe your nose.* He had a big white ring from coke around his nostril. She didn't want him to get pulled over with that booger sugar indicator.

He peeled out of the driveway in the lunky sports car, it looked so oddly dated. She'd never seen one up close. There had been a coffee house in Chicago that had a fake DeLorean from Back to The Future hanging from the ceiling, but that was her only interaction with the infamous car. As she closed the door and locked it- she decided to drain the tub and get the hell out of here, incase this unsavory guys friends showed up.

Quickly she tossed back on her clothes, drained the tub, replaced the gross plunger…but kept the knife, just in case anyone was out by the car. Flipping off the lights and the music she rocketed back out to Neil's Firebird and burned some Rockford Files rubber to get the hell out of there. She had reset the alarm… why did she feel she forgot something. "Oh shit, my bathing suit," she shook her head. Forget it, she wasn't going back.

She also had the bag from the guy in her pocket. It was heavy.
All the way back to the boat she kept checking her review mirror but no one was following her. When she hit the twinkling lights of Honolulu she breathed a sigh of relief and slowed down.

Back at La Mariana Sailing Club she parked her car and headed to the boat. The creaky dock seemed a bit more mysterious as she walked quickly. The Tube Top lady from the other night popped out of nowhere, "Hi!" she said.

Lucy almost jumped in the water, "Ha-hi," Lucy responded back, with a squeak.
"Everything Ok," the lady asked.

"Fine, fine, you just startled me," Lucy laughed nervously.
"Ok…well have a nice night."

"Yeah, you too!"

Back in the boat she turned on the cabin light, and took the mesh bag from her pocket. *Holy shit*…she gasped, looking at the sparkling contents, this was a lot of jewelry, really nice jewelry. Lucy's eyes were wide and she sifted through the contents, spreading it out on the plastic placemat. Bulgari, Chopard…a bunch of antique pieces, wow, a pink looking diamond…was it a diamond? This stuff was top-shelf. Then there was a key, she used her cell phone and held the Google Lens over it, hum, it was for a plane.

A knock at her door made her scrape the stuff back into the bag and she tossed it into the nearest trash can, no one would look there, she thought.

"Yes," she called out.

"Hey, it's me again, want to come over for a night cap, I won't take no for an answer." That Tube Top lady was beginning to be a pest.

"Ya know I'm seriously pooped," she said, peeking from behind the door.

"Awe come on, you gotta meet this real cool old guy- used to work for all these royal people and even Doris Duke…he has stories for days."

That woman knew exactly the right thing to say, "Hold on," Lucy moved the trash to the bathroom and crushed up a maxi pad so it looked used, and put it right on the top. No one would think to look here, she thought, feeling confident as she locked up.

Chapter 13

Next morning 9 a.m. sharp Neil was shipshape for his Wacky Weed Cruise. Jenny was happy he had found something to do while she was working.

Before bed she reminded him, "Just don't forget our dinner tomorrow night, you're going to meet my boss. Don't be late." He assured her he'd be back in plenty of time.

They began the boat trip with a little shoreline fishing and some ice-cold beer. After a shitty night's sleep on the bed that begged to roll him off at every move, the soothing hot sun and perfect ocean breeze were beginning to cure his negative attitude.

"Do you like reggae music? I got some Bob Marley and Roots of Reggae Mix. Also something called Legalize It Mix," Haku suggested.

"Let's go for the Legalize Mix, shall we," Neil suggested, kicking back and lighting up a spliff from his "little friend."

He couldn't believe no one else was up for this, he was the only guy on this cruise. Stew would've been here in a heartbeat if Neil had invited him. Thankfully Stew was none the wiser, probably sleeping off his hangover. He had heard Jenny leave at the crack of dawn. He didn't know how she did what she did—it was a difficult job and it didn't always reward long hours and hard work like he would've demanded, but she was as loyal as they come. The government was lucky to have her. The kid had assured him they would be back by 3 p.m., so he'd have time to shower and look presentable before meeting Jenny's boss.

"Where did you get this smoke?" Neil asked the boy, whose name was Haku.

Haku gave him a sheepish grin, flashing his bright white smile against his tan Polynesian skin. "Ask me no questions I tell you no lies."

They talked about music and school. The more the kid talked, Neil felt like something wasn't adding up. "How old are you, Haku?"

Again Haku blushed and looked guilty. "If I tell you, you will be shocked."

Neil did suddenly feel a bit nervous. He really hadn't thought this trip through—with the exception of escaping Stew and "Mrs. Smails," his focus was solely on getting away.

"I'm in high school . . . um, I just turned seventeen."

Neil almost choked on his beer. "Oh shit, kid, am I gonna get arrested for corrupting a minor?" Neil took a big nervous drag off the spliff, sweat suddenly beading his brow.

"Hey, you didn't know, I ditched school to sell you weed on my dad's boat."

True, the kid had misled him, insinuating he was a young business professional.

Then it hit reality hit Neil once again, "DAD'S BOAT!! Jeeeeesus kee-rist," Neil said, almost falling off his seat. "I could be looking at jail time."

Neil was now fully alarmed. He had extinguished his fun-sized doobie in the makeshift ashtray—a ceramic plate with an animated smiling jolly crab captain reaching up with its claw, 3-D style, so its pinchers could grip a cigarette or in this case, a soggy joint. On the plate was some cursive writing that said, "No Worries—No Problem."

The boat was really moving now. The Clash came blaring out of the Legalize It Mix—"I fought the law and the law won"—and Haku was letting the boat accelerate right into a massive wave. The boat lurched and Neil's beer went flying onto the floor and rolling like a torpedo being launched out of the back end of the boat, hurtling past him as it ricocheted off the cooler and into the ocean.

"Don't worry, Neil," the sneaky little degenerate consoled him. "It's all good, man. Wait until you see this secret island! You will be glad that this young entrepreneur brought you out here."

"Do you realize how many laws I'm breaking here?" Neil could feel his palms becoming sweaty.

"Shoulda thought about that before you smoked the wacky tobacky!" Mr. Smart-Ass replied, smiling and trying to look in control of the situation.

"You little shit." Now Neil scoffed, trying to stand tall and ominous, hovering over Junior Achievement. Neil gave the key a yank and cut the engine, the music and the boat coming to an abrupt halt. He had to let the kid know he was boss.

"Let's get something straight—we go to the island, then head back. You get your money and don't pull any more funny stuff." Neil thought the boy would jab back with an "or what," but instead he nodded in approval.

"If you like it will you tell more people. I've got college to pay for."

"You are shitting me, right?" Neil gazed at the watery horizon. He was at a nautical disadvantage here. He didn't know where the hell he was and he was high as fuck. The kid had laid some strong-ass weed on him. They'd gotten this far, maybe he should just enjoy the ride.

The kid began to restart the boat. "No, bruddah, no kidding here—I want to make money! I've got big plans. I want to own a company like this someday. You are like my prototype!"

Neil sighed. This kid reminded him of himself. How many schemes had he run by the age of sixteen . . . not to mention forty-three?

The boat motor gurgled, but it did not turn over. The kid kept talking, but something that looked like worry passed over his young confident face.

Haku said, "Why'd you have to pull the key? I think the emergency shutoff got triggered." He said this nervously as he kept trying to restart the engine. The boat was rocking, but the sounds of the ocean that had replaced the music now seemed vast and menacing. The boat was now a watery rocking pendulum, swinging between very serious mature waves. Lucky this was a pretty large boat—it easily could've fit twelve people or more, it wasn't gonna flip, he rationalized trying to sooth his nerves.

Haku checked his coordinates and actually pulled a laminated map from the top hidden compartment above the steering wheel. Neil also noticed some kind of flare gun in there and made note of it.

Haku explained, "We have a GPS, depth finder, and electric map. I even have a marine VHF radio, but nothing seems to be working." Haku now looked utterly baffled that technology had failed him. He kept punching in codes and trying to talk on the handheld orange waterproof-looking walkie-talkie. "It's set to channel 16, it's the distress signal." He gave the handheld device to Neil helplessly.

For a moment Neil looked out onto the ocean, trying to compose himself. Underneath his big strong exterior was the heart of quivering puppy. Give him a bar fight and he could handle it . . .

but with miles of strong ocean currents and waves chucking around this big seacraft like a little toy, he was feeling weak in the knees.

"Let's take a look at that map," Neil suggested. They went under the cover of the boat to get away from the whipping wind. It was still sunny but the weather was fickle.

Neil recalled his dad saying, "Bring me solutions, not problems," so that's what they had to do.

He cracked open another beer and then took a pull from his flask filled with tequila from last night. *Two-Fisted Tales*, he thought ironically. Who would believe this shit would keep happening to him? Did he piss someone off when he went to Haiti last year? Had they put a voodoo curse on him?

"Can I have a sip of that?" Haku asked.

"Absolutely fuckin' not." Neil looked at the kid hard and long and then back at the map, trying to let the fog from his smoky brain clear. "Do you know where we are, Haku?"

"Yes," Haku replied, exasperated. "That's what I've been trying to tell you. We are super-close to Disappearing Island. I'm sure there's a shack there with a CB radio. That's where a bunch of us were stashing and growing weed last year."

"Do you have a skiff and paddles?" Neil asked.

Haku puckered up his face like he smelled a fart. "Why you have to talk that way, brah? Yes, I gotta inflatable lifeboat."

So off they went like Gilligan and the Skipper; who was who was anyone's guess. The waves were pushing the little dingy like a bully on the playground but between him and Haku he could see this little island the kid was talking about, Disappearing Island.

"So, Haku, why do they call it Disappearing Island?" he asked. Neil's arms were already beginning to ache as he pumped the oars toward the island and his lungs burned, reminding him he smoked a lot of weed daily.

The kid explained how it had disappeared after a terrible typhoon. "Like one day we were going out here to get high and party, a week later the storms just buried it, gone like it never existed. Then, I heard some fishermen talking, scaling fish at the docks, saying how it had just reappeared, boom, a year later, the place is back."

He paused for a second and they just sort of floated. The waves had calmed down and the sun was back. He went on, "There's trees and jungle, you would never know it was gone! Since it came back somebody put like, a shack and some propane tanks and stuff out there, no one lives there for sure, I mean it's really small. I've only been a couple times since it reappeared. But it's cool. You find skeletons from the sea, things that have washed up and died, maybe. Gives it a creepy cool feel."

He had a very reassuring way about him, this kid. He was smart and scrappy.

As they approached the island, to Neil's chagrin he saw some sharks congregating right beneath their dingy—in the clear, clean water they were swimming among themselves, nine footers, hopefully just nurse sharks or something. He and the boy closed in on the shore and heard the strangely reassuring sound of birds.

"See that little bird," Haku said, pointing. "It's a Tinian Monarch, people thought the military wiped them out, then someone saw them out here. No one wants to tell because then a bunch of people will come to this island and it won't be ours anymore."

Neil nodded. "Your secrets safe with me."

From a distance the beach looked multicolored and beautiful, but as Neil and Haku coasted up onto the sand and shells, Neil realized the multicolored bits were disposable lighters, broken bits of fishing gear, tangled barely visible fishing net and other high-density plastic crap. A blue crab poked its head out of a cold cream jar to usher them into a pensive greeting and then skuttled away.

Neil and the kid took a moment to compose themselves and take a look around at this remote paradise. Neil was not a religious guy, but for him, nature was God and God was nature. He respected it and feared it, but also had deep affection for the land. That's why he hoped never to leave the islands. At the same time, being lost out here was not what he had bargained for when he had signed up for this day excursion. They pulled the dingy up into the bushes so it wouldn't slide back into the ocean and really leave them screwed.

They began to walk and the sun decided to give them the full weight of its intense rays, but they slyly slipped into the lush, green vegetation. "It's not far, I think they put the gear deeper inland so if storms come up it won't be wiped away . . . unless there's another severe storm."

As they walked deeper into the island's belly, Neil heard a strange hissing or croaking.

"There's no animals here, right?" Neil asked almost rhetorically, knowing there were no animals on these tiny islands.

"No, not unless someone brought them. I mean, I heard some stupid kid at school say he saw something attack a seal here, but Ailani is full of shit. Seals will come and sun themselves on the shore, but what could eat them onshore?" The kid snorted, like it was the dumbest thing he'd ever heard.

But Neil couldn't help shake the feeling something had its eyes on them. That maybe they were being followed. He tried to listen when the kid finally shut up, but all he heard was the rub of his overpriced boat shoes digging into the moist cool sand. The air was so pure and fresh, like after a spring rain. He took in a deep lungful, smiling to himself, thinking this would be a story his sister would enjoy. This whole crazy "Three-Hour Tour" . . . luckily their

"Minnow" was anchored so it was just a matter of getting someone out here to jump-start their boat.

He could imagine himself telling Lucy about the "uncharted island," explaining that there was no Ginger or Mary Ann. His mind began to wander until he rolled his ankle and went down hard. "Fuck," he cursed.

Haku looked concerned, "You OK, brah?"

He rubbed his ankle and rotated it, yeah, it was OK. Just then he heard that sound and the kid heard it too. It was a terrifying sound, like a wet panther growling. He also distinctly heard someone say, "*We have visitors.*"

Neil snatched the kid's wrist and took off, but he didn't get very far before he saw a gigantic crocodile, with its pointy snout wide open, panting like a dog but thankfully chained up.

"Stop right there, get down on the ground, now!" a man's voice yelled, coming up behind them.

"I got 'em," he called to another guy, who came out of nowhere. Both guys were aiming shotguns at Neil and Haku.

"Did I fuckin' tell you to get up?" The blond surfer guy in cutoff jean shorts kicked Neil in the small of his back into the sand. Haku lay flat and turned his head to look at Neil, scared shitless.

"So what have we got here?" Both the men were about six feet tall and as leathery tanned as they come. One guy had some purple zinc oxide on his nose, and a long-sleeves white moisture wicking-shirt that read "Vineyard Vines" down the sleeve, and the cutoff shorts guy had no shirt at all but a big tattoo the size of a kid's Halloween mask of a Madonna and Child in the center of his chest. Mr. Cutoffs had an accent, too.

Neil spoke quickly. "Our boat just needs jump, and we can be on our way," he said, tasting the sand and attempting not to eat a mouthful while he explained.

"Yes . . . bad luck for you . . . we cannot do that." The Russian-sounding guy with the big tattoo spat.

"This blows, Pavel, seriously blows," Rick the preppie surfer whined, still pointing his gun Neil's way, his purple zinc oxide nose twitching. He looked at Pavel for answers. If the guy didn't look so desperate, it might have been funny.

The tattooed Russian answered calmly, "It's not a problem, we fix it, we forget it."

Neil said nothing, trying to figure out his next move. He had a pretty good idea that he and Haku were dead meat unless they got away. The Pavel guy seemed like he was ready to shoot them He seemed a bit more psychotic then Rick the surfer dude—he was probably the owner of the croc, which seemed to now be dozing off in the shade.

Neil spoke again. "We have no idea where we are, but my wife works for the military. They will expect us back by sundown."

Both the men laughed in a threatening, guttural way, giving Neil an alarming sense of hopelessness. These obvious criminals were not even going to offer salvation—they were just figuring out how to kill them and not leave a trace.

Neil hoped if they thought he and the kid were lost maybe they'd dump them on another island.

The men dragged them to their feet roughly. The kid was hanging tough, no tears and no begging. He knew these men meant business.

They walked past the chained-up, now awake croc, which was trying to snap at them and break its chain. The men laughed uncontrollably. "Maybe you feed Oscar tonight? He's hungry boy, and he's in a bad mood since you woke him from his nap." Pavel suddenly grabbed the kid's hand. "Want to pet the nice crocodile?"

"NO," Neil screamed, sounding none too threatening and all too hysterical. He tried to break away and got the butt of the gun in the gut. He doubled over, almost losing his lunch.

"Oh, Mr. Big Protector. What are you two doing out here? You gays?" Pavel spat.

The kid spoke quickly, he seemed calmer than Neil, the folly of youth. "He's my sister's boyfriend, I was showing off my dad's boat and we got lost."

Nice bullshitting, Neil thought.

"Well, ya fucked up, kid," said a new guy. He was stocky but extremely fit, his hair was sun streaked but you could tell he was dark haired. He wore an old frayed red aloha shirt and well-worn blue board shorts with "Haleiwa Hotel" emblazoned on them.

There was a small makeshift shack behind him and two people with gas masks came out, wearing slippery-looking chef's smocks, like they were at a chemistry cookout.

When Neil took a deep breath and looked around at the trash cluttering their camp area, the chemical stink all made sense. Neil eyeballed what seemed like hundreds of boxes of Wal-fed, Sudafed, Claritin, Coricidin, and Aprodine boxes. He shook his head, *no one had a cold here*. There were corroded rubber tubes, coffee filters, big mason jars with rusty metal tops, and bowls strewn about all over what should have been a slice of pristine paradise. Instead, these losers had turned the island into a meth lab for cooking drugs. The ammonia stench burned his nostrils—it almost smelled like paint varnish. The cookers, who'd just removed their gas masks, also seemed highly agitated.

The skinny one in a bathing suit tore off her smock. "Why are they here, why are they alive, what the fuck are you two here for . . . you bring them here . . . you stupid pieces of shit." She should have been beautiful with her long sun-washed hair down to her butt and the tightest, ropiest hard body Neil had seen since the last Quicksilver surf competition, but as she came up to him and got into his face, aggressive as hell, she was like a pockmarked psycho banshee. As she nearly spit in his face, her red bloodshot eyes mad with a ferocious chemical rage, he wondered if she was going to bite off his face.

Meth was an ugly drug. People always want to watch these zombie apocalypse movies . . . well, go to a party where everyone is tweeking and the experience is palpable. Neil sure as shit was not up for that twitchy-ass high, no thanks, he'd prefer to keep his teeth and not look like an extra on *The Walking Dead*. Yet here he was in the center of his own horror flick!

The Russian and Rick poked them with their guns toward a couple of Porta Potties that were bungeed together. *Neil was not feeling good about this at all*. He hated meth almost as much as he hated portable toilets.

The bad guys took Neil and Haku separately, pushing Neil into the men's toilet stall and Haku into the women's stall, locking them in. Hotter than hell was the first impression besides the aroma of rotting shit and something more sinister. There was a rag with some brown stuff that didn't look like shit sitting by the opening of the toilet. Something made Neil cover his face with his T-shirt and peer inside. He almost screamed and puked when he spotted the half-decomposed head staring at him with bugs swarming all over it.

Puke was not a choice at this point. He heaved a huge amount of vomit, eyes watering. He could hear Haku whisper through the vent, "You OK, brah?"

Neil paused, and something fierce and deep took over inside of him. They would not end up in the shitter with fucking bugs breeding in their brains, *aw hell no*. He began making his plan. But first he took the last of the toilet paper scraps, rubbed them in his sweaty armpits, and rolled them into little balls, shoving them in his nostrils—anything was better them smelling rotting body and rancid shit.

Chapter 14

She watched the water slowly and rhythmically drip off the eaves of the boat. The day was overcast again and the rain seemed like it was here to stay. She had some Cambodian Highlife music, Lion Progressive Club- smooth jazz playing and was reading a graphic novel about traveling in Indo-Chinese Peninsula.

Cambodia had so many beautiful relics that were deteriorating in the humid climate. Thailand, Laos, Vietnam and Cambodia were on her list of places to go to. She really believed the best way to know a culture is to know its music. It was a door opener.

In Central Park last year a guy was driving her and Amanda around in a pedicab and when Lucy found out he was from Nigeria, she got really excited and put her iPhone on speaker and played some Nigerian Highlife, a funk/rock/jazz fusion with incredible musicianship. He got so excited, and started sharing stories about his homeland and upbringing. What a ride!

As she looked out her little window at the palm fronds so unconcerned about the rain, she remembered a time long ago when she'd lie on her family's boat in Michigan, floating in the hot summer sun, unconcerned, drifting, and peaceful, much like those palm fronds. . . . She was far away from her thirteen-year-old self now. She switched her iPod to the Police and now, when she closed her eyes, she was almost back there, like she'd stepped into a musical time machine. Instead of the Michigan waves she was being cradled to and fro by the South Pacific. She was so terribly glad to be here, this island was medicinal for what ailed her. She said a short thank-you prayer to her dad—without him Neil wouldn't even be here and neither would she.

Then her phone tinged. She looked at the clock on the wall and thought it would be too late for Amanda, and her brother was not addicted to his phone like she was. Anyway, he'd be busy.

She played ping-pong with her mind as to whether she should reengage with the world.

"Ting, ting, ting, ting, ting . . ." Oh, lord, she thought. She rolled her eyes. She didn't like the sound of all of those text messages.

Her phone was plugged in but had fallen onto the floor of the boat and was lying belly up on the shaggy worn hunk of a harvest-yellow bath mat that was next to the bed. She flipped it over to see the screen. The first text was Guy, her agent.

TEXT 1: You forgot to initial page 4, please do so or I can't proceed with negotiations.

TEXT 2: Ashly Martin would really like a one-on-one, could you agree to FaceTime her?

TEXT 3: She said she could wait. But I think you should strike while the iron's hot, she's been listening to your podcast. Loves it.

Lucy cringed. Her podcast was just goofy stuff. She was trying to teach herself how to edit music using the computer and pretending to be a DJ after binge-watching *WKRP in Cincinnati.* **Lunatic Fringe**, stories from the edges of music and media. That was the premise for her "show." She had never learned how to edit so it was basically her talking and playing weird songs from her music collection. Not something she wanted Ashly Martin to hear.

Now all these people were hearing her music reviews, book critiques, and Lucy smack talking about current events. This was embarrassing.

TEXT 4: Wait until you see this contract I am drafting, you will shit bricks! You can perform the songs too. Not everyone can do that, ya know. You may be able to buy a condo by your brother by the time I'm done.

Lucy smiled in the twilight. Hummm, that did sound good.

TEXT 5: Hi Lucy, I don't want to alarm you, but I think your brother is missing. Please call me! Jenny.

HOLY SHIT!

Lucy almost dropped her phone as she speed-dialed her sister-in-law. Jenny picked up right away.

Lucy had never heard Jenny so flustered. She was always so calm and collected. "Hey, girl . . . so, we've got a problem and it's kind of sticky. I'm scared."

"OK, tell me what's up." Lucy realized she was shaking.

"So your brother went on a boat cruise this morning at 9 a.m. and he was supposed to be back at 3 p.m., so when he didn't return to the hotel room I went down to the pier. Here's where it gets weird. The guys who rents out the boats doesn't know what I'm talking about. They only saw a couple privately owned boats go out at that time."

Lucy could hear her start to cry.

"Oh, honey, it's going to be OK."

"So I told the guys who are close to me here, they are special forces guys, I had to go to them because—there's a glitch, Neil told me it's a Weed Cruise. He's on some kind of day trip where marijuana is involved and it's illegal on the island and . . . .I could lose my job. It's not like civilian life. . . ."

Lucy could barely understand Jenny through her tears.

Lucy suggested, "Hey, I've got an idea. It's early here. Why don't I run up and see if I can find Jimmie Jay, the guy I'm renting the boat from. He's a retired cop. Maybe we can cruise up there and look for him."

"Lucy, it's like almost 2,500 miles away. You'd have to fly up here and rent a boat."

Lucy paused for a second. "Just get me some tickets and we will be there."

"OK, I can do that! Meanwhile, my Special Forces guys will be out there looking but if you come we can bullshit and say it's just vacation stuff. The guys are doing it on the down low for now. It would be great if you were here."

Lucy hung up and threw on some comfortable clothes and ran in the rain up to the bar at La Marina. Tuna was calling as she locked up the boat and she texted him, "My brother's in trouble on the Kwajalein Islands, his tour boat's lost or something, I'll text ya later."

Tuna replied, "I know people there, just say the word if ya need help."

The bar at La Marina Sailing Club was pretty empty, just a few regulars nursing Bloody Marys. "Hi, is Jimmie Jay here?" she asked one of the waitresses, a skinny older woman more in shape than Lucy would ever be.

"Somewhere . . . maybe he's in the can, he'll be out in a minute. Go wait up there, he'll show up." Lucy was glad she'd called his emergency number and his sister explained he was at the bar. How convenient!

Lucy took a seat at the bar. There was a big fish tank behind the counter on the back wall surrounded by fully stocked shelves of booze.

The fish tank was a pièce de résistance in terms of an aquatic interior. Multicolored fish of various sizes and shapes darting back and forth among the unnaturally glowing neon coral, the swaying murky sea grasses shifting back with the flick of their fishy tails it had an eerie mysterious quality.

If La Marina Sailing Club didn't spell TIKI Lucy didn't know what did. Behind her she could hear the splash from the man-made waterfalls inside volcanic rock grottoes that were sporting some mighty fine Hawaiian, Tahitian, and Polynesian sculptures. The plants grew full and lush from every pot and crevice surrounding the intimate booths. This would be a good Valentine's Day spot, she thought, she wishing Amanda was here—she was good at bringing order to chaos. Lucy was the big sister and she was gonna reel Neil back in, whatever it took. She tried to call Amanda but got a message saying the circuits were busy. What the hell?

"Whats-choo want, Lucy." Jimmie Jay looked a bit harried. He had mis-buttoned his aloha shirt, which was obviously his bartending shirt and was stained with some of last night's drink specials.

"I've got a serious situation, Jimmie Jay."

His eyes got wide and he looked ready to shoot smoke out of his nostrils like an angry bull. "You fuck up my boat, didn't choo???"

"No, no, nothing like that." She shook her head.

He looked massively relieved.

"My brother is missing and I thought maybe since you were a retired police officer, you could help."

He put his hands on his skinny hips, and then thinking better of it, lit up a cigarette. No one in the restaurant batted an eye.

"You know what retired means . . . ?"

"Yes, I know, but I thought maybe you could help. We are in a pickle because my sister-in-law is doing some work she can't talk about for the military and now my brother went out on a boat and it hasn't come back."

"Lucy, Lucy, Lucy . . . you think I'm Hawaii Five-0 or some shit? I retired, I hated being a cop and I tell you I didn't leave the department in good standing. I'm a legacy, that was my curse. . . ."

"Your dad?"

He snorted. "Oh, honey . . . uncles, dads, brothers . . . ya know who Chang Apana is?" He gave Lucy a long hard look while she racked her brain.

"Wait a minute." She was suddenly over-the-moon excited. "You mean Charlie Chan!"

"Charlie-Fuckin'-Chan, his real name was Chang Apana, but they call all Asians Charlie back in those days. Real 'Chan' get hit by a car then they demote him to a watchman in a bank. This was a guy who they took his life and made millions. He dies of gangrene, that's some bullshit."

"Oh, Jimmie, I didn't know." She felt guilty for loving all the Charlie Chan movies, he was her underdog, her hero. He beat the odds, but that was the movies.

Jimmie Jay eased up and explained, "I mean you gotta let that shit go, the guy died in '33 but then all those boy children gotta go and be cops too. Since I didn't have no aspirations my parents *force the force* on me, ya know. Hell, I like bartending better." The two drunks at the bar waved when they heard this—it wasn't like Jimmie was quiet. He was bellowing this story quite loudly.

"I will pay you if you help me," she said, trying to persuade him.

He raised an eyebrow. "If I say yes, I look like a lowlife . . . but a guy's gotta pay his slip fees."

He crushed out his cigarette in an old mother-of-pearl iridescent abalone shell ashtray.

Her phone had been vibrating while they were talking. "My sister-in-law just emailed me tickets, she said we can go to Bellows, a little airport on the north side of the island, and they will know to expect us."

He gave Lucy a funny look. "Who's your sister-in-law? That's an Air Force base in Waimanalo—Department of Defense."

"It's by the old Magnum P.I. place, right?"

He drew up his hands dramatically. "See, just when I'm getting to like you, you say some stupid haole thing like that . . . geez."

"So you are gonna help me?"

"Yeah, a girl alone, sure. But I'm taking time off for work, so ya know."

"Pay . . . yes, I know. We will have to figure it out."

He called over the waitress. "Tell Chuck he gotta cover, family emergency," he said

She looked at them dubiously but nodded.

"We take your hot rod, I'm not losing my sweet parking spot," he said as he and Lucy walked to her brother's Sierra Gold Firebird. He of course insisted on driving. Lucy didn't care; he knew his way around better than she did.

Behind the wheel he was like a kid in a candy store. "Oh, this baby is mint. Some guys want Italian sport car when they are kids, no, no, not me. I like this Firebird. This is cool ride."

He was driving like a cop on assignment, plowing through the streets and scaring the crap out of Lucy.

They got to Bellows in record time. "This place was hot shit in World War II, I don't know what they're doing here now but I got laid on this beach right over there." He pointed off to the right, where a large weepy mangrove tree stood against the backdrop of a long luscious beach scape. He explained, "Civilians can come here, just not through the gate." He pointed up ahead, to make his point. A guard in fatigues was turning people away.

When Jimmie Jay approached he was very professional and he and Lucy handed the guard their identification. The guard who looked like a tough guy, not someone who could be schmoozed, gave them the hard look and called someone. Then a few minutes later he waved them through, watching them all the way down the road.

The waiting plane was what Lucy would call a puddle jumper. For some reason, she figured they would be in a helicopter. She realized she hadn't packed any clothes.

They were ushered in with a few other uniformed officers and it made her nervous. But no one said anything. They got seated in a very utilitarian plane, nothing that would have a fancy flight attendant, not the most glamorous four hours she would spend on a plane, but it was free.

It didn't hurt that Jimmie Jay Choi was a former cop.

Jenny had stressed that they should give as little information as possible and just tell anyone who asked that Lucy and Jimmie Jay were visiting family for vacation.

Lucy took a snooze, Jimmie was playing a game on his phone. By the time she awoke they were almost there.

Jenny met Lucy and Jimmie at the air strip. She filled them in on what she knew. Her guys were still out looking. "I rented you a boat with navigation, food, drinks, laptop, GPS/depth finder. If you guys can't find him by tomorrow, I'll just let the command know and take my chances. Sergeants Smyth and Campbell are my friends who are looking for them, they think there is a very good chance the boat he's on just punked out and they are adrift. . . but there are a lot of islands around here. They could've drifted in a million different directions. The fact no radar has spotted them is really strange. I mean really strange." She looked worried and her face was tight. "I'm going to go back to work like everything is fine." She got up from the table in the Kwaj Lodge, where we were all having iced tea, trying to act casual. "We are on a deadline."

Jenny dropped them off at the boat and luckily Jimmie was still in professional mode. Lucy hopped aboard the big **Sea Ray**, which looked like a glamorous fishing craft. Jimmie Jay was busy taking orders from the marina captain, who was saying, "She's got you checked out until six." The rental guys showed Jimmie Jay and Lucy around and then they signed some papers.

"Don't get lost out there!" the rental guy laughed.

"No problem, I spend some time on **Ebeye Island**, we install a soccer field for the kids to play when I was with the force," Jimmie Jay told the rental guy.

When they got out on open waters Lucy asked, "What's Ebeye Island?"

"Ever been to Haiti?" he asked, steering the huge powerful boat into the endless watery horizon.

"No . . ."

"Ebeye is kinda like Haiti. It's a poverty-stricken community our government polluted the shit out of then," he explained with more than a little sarcasm in his voice, "Was like, see ya later. Most of the island is under the age of eighteen, something like that. They don't got shit so we went out to help install some sports stuff for the kids. Really, really sweet people. It tears me up seeing that kind of need, ya know. Not right, not right at all."

They were driving in the direction Jimmie thought a "cruise" might go. "I wonder if he's with other people?" Jimmie asked, "I mean no one else was reported missing?"

"Possibly a kid took him out on the boat, Jenny said it was so he could go smoke some weed and get away from Stew and this Colonel's Wife."

"Who's Stew?" he asked suspiciously.

"He's some real estate guy, big bragger."

"Oh, honey, say no more. My ex-wife was a broker. That's why I live in a boat, fuck her." One thing about Jimmie, he was very animated. Lucy could imagine him doing some sort of stand-up.

The sun was so overbearing at this time of day it put them into a quiet lull. They traveled around some small islands and atolls. Lucy was surprised how well Jimmie knew the area. He snickered, "I'm not that good, I gotta map right here," he said, patting the electronic dashboard. She would've really been enjoying the sightseeing if it wasn't for her brother being lost. She tried not to get too dramatically terrified. The what-if's were the very worst in a creative mind like hers.

They had slowed down because something had caught Jimmie's eye, "Oh, momma . . . I don't know if I want to tell you this." He was sort of snickering.

"Well out with it, geez," she said, annoyed, getting up from the white vinyl swivel seat and peering at his dashboard.

"See that?" He pointed to the monitor.

She looked over his bony shoulder at the radar screen only to see a huge moving thing beneath the boat. "Is it a sub?"

"Hahaha, nope. We got Jaws hanging out right below us. Man, I wish I knew how to take photographs with this boat, that is one big fishy."

Her already-scared self hit a Mach 5 heart rate. She looked at the "fish," which was "three times the size of their boat," she exclaimed, horrified. She began to tremble involuntarily. It pissed her off to be this scared.

"Not quite that big, Lucy," he replied, "but it's a good eighteen feet, I'm gonna guess a female. The guys don't get that big, usually." He didn't seem too worried, so she took it as her cue to try and calm down.

"I want to get closer to that island here," he pointed back at the digital map. "I got a feeling, this current . . . the winds . . . they all seem to be going over there," he said, nodding toward a far-off tiny-looking speck of a green mass. As it came up closer and quicker, there seemed to be a ring-shaped coral reef that encircled a lagoon. Normally she would've wanted to get off the boat and swim just to cool off—the water looked so clean and clear and it had gotten so broiling hot. They had already been out a few hours and she needed to pee. Jaws wasn't on the radar any longer.

"We can stop off, when we get to where I want to go, it's just about another twenty minutes, can you hold it?"

She felt slightly embarrassed. "Oh yeah, sure!" She refreshed her spray sunscreen and cracked open a Coke. She'd already had two bottles of water and munched on some chips.

The small island Jimmie had been talking about came into view. "OK, now I don't want to freak you out. . . ." He was biting his thumbnail.

"YOU saying that freaks me out."

"This island is off the map, in fact it disappeared—wiped off the map after a powerful hurricane swept through here—but the fucker reemerged, I was told." He sighed. "OK, this is probably made up, but Nary, my brother-in-law," he repeated, "is a sport fisherman, real bragger, probably like that Stew guy. He said they saw some monk seals and shit out here, and then there was like a huge commotion, and he swears, swears"—Jimmie looked pretty serious—"he swears he saw a saltwater croc eat one of the monk seals, like taking it down, man." Jimmie had become very high-spirited again, like this was a campfire story and he was trying to scare a bunch of little kids, but he was only succeeding in scaring Lucy.

Lucy was flabbergasted. "You think my brother got eaten by a croc?" she almost squeaked, a pinched cry leaping from her voice.

"Oh, shit, no. I meant, if I was taking someone on a cool tour, giving them their money's worth, I'd take them to an island very few people knew existed and had cool stories attached. Tourists love that shit."

Lucy felt slightly better but then the thought of her brother getting chowed on by a gigantic saltwater crocodile made her eyes start to well up and put a lump in her throat.

"Let's go back, Jimmie, tell the authorities. I feel bad for Jenny, she'll lose her job and they'll have to move back to the mainland, but I don't want my brother to die." She was dead serious.

Jimmie scoffed, "Listen you got me on this case and now I want to finish it, we gonna find your big stupid haole brother in one piece and bring him back to Kwaj. Then we go have some sizzling Korean ribs at **Sorabol**." His big wide smile and the pat he gave Lucy on the shoulder, which now felt sunburnt, somehow comforted her. "We can do this, Lucy." He looked serious and she felt a renewed sense of commitment.

"If we got trouble I noticed a few flare guns," Lucy said weakly.

"Now, that's the spirit!" He was nodding vigorously as he pulled closer to the creepy dark shore.

It was strange standing on a vacant shore, feeling a cool breeze. The shade felt as heavy as a tent covering yet beckoned them inside it's leafy lair. Seeing her brother's empty boat anchored offshore felt like a bad omen and any security she had slipped away. She tried to shake off this bad feeling she had. They had taken a little dingy to the island. Maybe they were just camping out since the boat had died.

"There's a lot of coral and rock underneath the water. It's safer this way," Jimmie explained as they pulled the small boat onto shore. Their dingy actually had navigation and a little kit of freeze-dried food and water.

They walked inward, toward the darkness of the tree cover. "There's no snakes . . . maybe spiders," Jimmie said.

"Do you have to keep doing that—making me feel safe for a second and then pulling out the safety net and adding something equally dangerous or creepy!" A sudden surge of backbone came back to her, and she felt her strength return. THINK JONNY QUEST! she said to herself. Who says TV doesn't enhance your life!

It was so dark under the canopy of trees that she would've thought it was night, but as they hiked through the underbrush, heavy sand and cracked shells, big strobes of light would flash from between the trees, alerting them it was still daylight.

After walking for awhile she smelled something funny in the air, something she couldn't put her finger on. "Hey, Jimmie, is it me or does it smell like Windex?" she whispered, not really knowing why. "*Jimmie . . .*"

She had looked away for a second and now all she heard was chirping. The trees around her rustled and her stomach began to flutter with nerves.

"*Jimmie, Jimmie,*" she called out, raising her voice stumbling along the heavy green growth, hoping there were no huge iron-shelled millipedes with their big pincers to bite her delicate toes. Her flip-flop caught the top of an open glass jar and she panicked as she tripped over a bunch of glass pickle jars that were piled in a shallow hole. Making a huge commotion, she paused. Thankfully she had caught herself on a tree trunk. Looking around, fury began to build—where was fucking Jimmie?

She thought she heard some voices and hope sprang into her heart. She sped up. Walking over some rusty car parts and almost cutting her foot open, she cursed beneath her breath and thought something was odd. Blue rust? Weird, she thought as she called out for Jimmie once more. Then a hand yanked her backward roughly. "*Shut up.*"

It was Jimmie and he looked worried. "We got problems." He began dragging her back to their boat.

"What, what is it . . . and where were you?"

"I'll tell you about it when we get on the boat." They were almost running and she felt they were taking a different path. "Hey, is this the same way?"

"Shut up and follow me, remember that sea croc I told you about?" he said, slightly winded as they approached the shore. "It's real, I saw the trail track! Let me tell you those bastards are patient, they can sit in the water for four hours just waiting for you to wade by in knee-deep water and then bam, you're in chow town and it's immediate damage. Good-bye, leg, good-bye arm."

They could see the dingy and ran toward it. She was following Jimmie blindly but she was no cop . . . she needed to just listen. They shoved off, hopping in and hoping not to lose a leg to the unseen predator.

They were back on the big boat fairly quickly.

Jimmie started up the engine and they began to take off. "There's someone there," she said. "But I don't think my brother was there," she added confidently.

"Wrong-o, he's there!"

"What!" she exclaimed excitedly. "let's get him now!" She was almost yelling at Jimmie, the wind and sea spray whipping her hair and face. She inhaled its bitter salt spray. "What the fuck, Jimmie!"

"Calm down, let me get us safe. I'll explain." He checked the radar screen and the time. The sun was setting and they had to get the boat back so they wouldn't cause any suspicion.

When they had passed the lagoon, Jimmie pointed for her to sit back down on the passenger-side swivel chair. "OK, did you smell that urine, ammonia smell."

She nodded.

"Lucy, that's the stink of a meth lab. Ya know, methamphetamines. These are bad dudes."

"All the more reason to go get my brother!"

"No, no, no—we need help. These guys are armed. I think that fuckin' croc is their guard dog, too. What are we gonna do, go in wearing our flip-flops with a couple of flare guns and tell them to fork over your brother and his little boat captain?"

She agreed that would be stupid.

"We need to talk to those Special Forces guys your sister-in-law is friends with. We need people who are trained to ambush these scum buckets, get your brother and the kid out safely."

She paused, having to pee again, fighting off the lump in her throat. "It's my baby brother, Jimmie."

Jimmie looked at her sternly. "Your six-eight baby brother is better off if we don't cause a commotion. I'm no Jim Rockford or Magnum, Lucy. This isn't a movie—it's your brother's life."

Just then her phone rang. She looked at the screen. "You've got to be fucking kidding me," Lucy said through teary eyes. She flashed the screen at Jimmie. Ashly Martin the pop singer was calling on FaceTime.

Chapter 15

Lucy didn't answer the FaceTime from Ashly Martin. That talk would have to wait.

Back on the deck of the Sea Ray, the boatThe boat was slapping the waves so hard she felt like her uterus was going to fall out. She actually buckled into the white vinyl swivel chair next to Jimmie Jay as they made their way over the choppy water to another boat.

"How do you know it's not bad guys?" she yelled over the boat's engine and the ocean's fury.

"Call letters—military. I hope it's your sister-in-law's friends." He made a face that didn't inspire confidence.

Sure enough, Jenny's "friends," Retrieval Red Team Sergeant Campbell and Sergeant Smyth were on the lookout from their boat and waved them down.

"Are you Lucy and Jimmie Jay?" the blond guy with a crew cut asked. "I'm Sergeant Campbell and this is Sergeant Smyth," he said, pointing to the other guy who looked a little more hip and scruffy.

Tethering the bobbing boats together, they hopped aboard the craft Jimmie Jay and Lucy were in and accepted a couple of bottles of water and some Snickers bars. Jimmie Jay gave them the lowdown.

"It's a drug operation," Jimmie Jay explained as they all caught each other up on the scoop. Jimmie Jay explained some of what he saw: "The one girl is out of her mind, she's sampling the goods for sure and I don't like her tone. There's three others including her."

The sergeant's shared their intel. "We found your brother's boat. Actually, it belongs to a Mr. Kahale. That's the father of boy who took your brother out under false pretenses, for his, um . . . cruise."

Smyth explained, "There's a dinghy on the other side of the island. I presume it's theirs but there was no sign of them along the coast, but we saw smoke."

Jimmie explained, "tThey are being held I believe in or around the cook house—it looks like an old streamline trailer. There's some makeshift Porta Potties and some fancy-looking tents.""

The boats were smacking together and just as quickly as the waves beat into them they had calmed down. Sergeant Smyth scratched his dark mass of unruly curls. "So how should we proceed? I'm thinking authorities."

"I'm thinking I have an idea," Lucy said. Everyone looked at her.

They all decided the sergeants should stay around the island to make sure no murder was going on. She needed to make some phone calls-but there was no reception way out here.

She and Jimmie Jay took the boat back like they had just had a lovely day out. The boat rental guy was none the wiser.

Jenny met them at the pier. "Check the boat out for tomorrow, 6 a.m.," Lucy told Jenny.

Lucy got on the horn and started calling some people. *First call was Tuna.*

"Tuna, it's Lucy, and I'm gonna cut to the chase, some fuckin' haole surfer dudes are cooking meth on this little island by Kwaj, and they have my brother and some kid he's with. Can you help? I know you mentioned the Hawaiian Harley bikers and the chapter head lives part-time on Kwaj. Could they help?"

Tuna was grunting and snorting as Lucy explained in more detail what Jimmie Jay saw, and she knew the fuse was lit. Jimmie Jay chimed in on speakerphone, and Lucy thought Tuna was going to explode on the phone. He was getting his Hawaiian warrior peck's pumping and it wasn't gonna be pretty.

"Pacific Bikers, all vets, and Ailani is my best bud . . . also Black Ops he will get in there and get your brother and the kid, those toxic fuckers are going down."

Over some very lackluster pizza at Anthony's, the only pizza joint on the island, Lucy explained to Jenny her plan about Tuna's posse. The Black Ops and Ailani were kind of known in her circle so she nodded warily.

The plan was that Campbell and Smyth would get the signal and retrieve Haku and Neil, getting them out safely, and then Ailani would go in with his brothers and "clean up" the mess. Ailani was hot, as in through-the-roof angry. Lucy spoke with him and he was so cool, calm, and enraged—"defiling our land, *contaminating our culture*, destroying our young people" were his exact words—oh, brother, this guy was a volcano and he was going to erupt all over these meth heads with a brotherhood of the toughest, smartest military bikers to hit the Micronesian Islands. Those surfers were gonna be sorry they had gone into the meth business and messed with this BIG SISTER!

The night was dark and even the strong ocean breeze couldn't cheer Lucy up as she, Jenny, and Jimmie Jay made their way back to the hotel.

Jenny explained, "You guys will be right next to my room, it's got twin beds and I got you some sweats from the PX, there's toiletries and stuff in the bathroom too."

As soon as the door to the hotel room shut Jimmie Jay exclaimed, "This place sucks."

"What did you expect, princess?" she sighed, taking in the landscape. Lime-green shag carpeting, two well-used twin beds that reeked of musty, moist, moldy storage room, and TV that was an old wood console that only got one channel on Polynesian living and island travel, no remote control needed.

There was Irish Spring soap and some Pantene shampoo and conditioner for dandruff. Was her sister-in-law trying to tell her something? Luckily the towels in the bathroom were for the beach so at least they covered more than just her butt. The sweats were thin and soft, actually very nice quality, and said "Army Strong" on the front.

Jimmie Jay did not want to wear his—they said "Military Brat" in neon green, with purple script. "I mean what happened here, this was really the only sweats in my size?"

"Dude, you are kinda small." She was trying not to laugh as he moped in his *oh-so-stylish* ensemble.

"See-Oh, see, *I see how you are*, judging me." Jimmie Jay snorted dramatically.

"I think she got me the wide load pants, so don't be so sensitive."

There were some extra beach towels in the closet so Lucy laid them over her bedding to try and not inhale the moldy perfume. She discovered Jimmie Jay was a snoring monster, and the room vibrated with his snorts until she fell into a fitful sleep.

The sun wasn't even up when Lucy smelled coffee. It seemed to be coming from the hall. She followed the trail, which led to her sister in law's room.

Jenny looked like she hadn't slept a wink. "Hi," Lucy said weakly as Jenny invited her in for some double-strong Starbucks.

"I bring my own, I live on it, don't you know!" Jenny explained.

Lucy took the chair by the desk and the coffee pot and Jenny sat on the bed. Jenny was already showered and ready to go.

"I'm telling the police if I don't see Neil by tonight." She exhaled deeply, like the weight of the world was weighing her down. "I should have dissuaded Neil from going on that cruise."

"You can't talk Neil out of anything. Don't beat yourself up, I'm sure he was hell-bent to get away from Stew." Lucy took a healthy swig of the hot, strong brew. "The authorities would normally be our best bet. But I'll tell ya, we basically have a better-trained force out there getting him back. I mean, high-ranking sergeants, Black Ops guys, and crazy-ass Hawaiian bikers . . ." Lucy paused for effect, "or the Keystone Cops around here—farting, eating Malasadas, with powdered sugar on their shirts, who would you want on your team?"

Jenny cracked the widest grin. "You just made me feel so much better, seriously." She paused and took a sip of her steaming coffee. "When I first met you we were kids, I didn't really like you," she said as if she were embarrassed.

"Feeling was mutual." Lucy nodded sheepishly.

"You were bouncing on your brother's bed one time, tossing condoms at him singing 'Neil's getting laid.'"

Lucy cringed, because she did remember. "I was an idiot big sister. I didn't know until later you were in the bathroom hiding."

They both laughed. "Now all these years later, there's no one I'd rather have right here with me than you." They both nodded. It was a bonding moment.

"Me too. You're more than a sister-in-law—you're a straight-up sister!"

There was a weak knock at the door. "I smell coffeee." The familiar voice of Jimmie Jay came from the hallway.

"It's none other than Charles in Charge," Lucy said, greeting a weary-looking Jimmie Jay. "Looking fresh in his Day-Glo best."

"Aw, screw you." He came in and poured himself a styrofoam cup of Starbucks French roast. "Got any Tum's? That half-assed pizza by Chef Boyardee is not sitting well in my gut."

Jenny popped up and got him some Rolaids.

"Thank you," he said kindly.

They chatted some more and then it was time to wrap things up.

"Hopefully, next time I see you two it will be with Neil."

Jimmie Jay, back to his professional best, albeit in neon green, nodded. "You can count on us."

Chapter 16

Neil closed the lid of the shitter, he tried to hold back the bile in the back of his throat but because of his stinking pits, he had to breathe through his mouth. He was gonna get out of this literal shit hole.

He peered out of the vents and could see in the distance the "scum brigade," four of them, all by what looked like a boat. The lights were on and it looked like they were settling in for the night. He easily popped the clasp on the door but there was a gold Master Lock, it wasn't latched but it was hooked in the holes from the outside. He just needed to flip it. . . . Searching around with his bare hand on the floor he hoped for a toilet paper roll or a pen, something long and firm.

He found it with a stabbing little prick to the pad of his index finger. "Oh, fuckin' great," he wheezed. "A used syringe." He almost freaked out thinking about getting AIDS or hep C or God knows what else, but it was the perfect tool for slipping between the door crack and lifting the lock right out of the holes.

Fresh air overcame his senses and he immediately felt a sense of renewed confidence—and rage, as his finger throbbed.

Quickly, Neil opened the other Porta Potty door for the kid. Haku fell out of the stall, hugging him awkwardly. "Thanks, brah."

They could hear the girl scream, "Who's gonna fuck me!" Haku and Neil looked at each other and grimaced with disgust.

"That broad has huffed one too many chemicals," Neil said, hearing her do another banshee screech into the quiet island night. It felt like a Rob Zombie horror movie.

"Ok, I think we gotta blow that cook shack," Neil said, pointing to the Airstream camper. " It will explode so big we will have time to grab our dinghy and get the fuck outta here."

"Sounds like a plan," Haku said, nodding vigorously.

"We need fire," Neil directed him. "Check some of those used lighters scattered around here and I'm gonna pour some of this foul chemical liquid around the trailer," Neil explained, grabbing a large pickle jar full of noxious chemical. If this wasn't flammable, he didn't know what was!

A few minutes later Haku came back. "I think this is one of those lighters you use for creme brûlée. . . ."

"Well, I'll be damned, it's a culinary lighter—full of butane. That will work, my young apprentice!"

Haku smirked, feeling proud.

The party was still full on when Neil leaned in to light the ring of fire. It torched up hot orange, and then blue and then . . . they ran, ran through the bush, down toward the shore as the screams and cursing began. Their little boat was waiting and they shoved off and were in the water. Bullets began flying and they knew these guys were coming after them. They had to get to their boat, but it was so dark. Haku found a handheld spotlight in the toolbox in the dinghy and was sweeping it in front of them. Then they realized they were ankle deep in water—the captors had cut holes in the dinghy, but it was still moving . . . in these shark-infested waters.

Haku screamed. One of the bullets had hit him.

For a moment Neil realized they could die out there, but he refused to give in.

"My ear, Neil, it's my ear. I think they just got the tip. I can hear . . . they're getting closer."

The water was really coming in and the boat was moving slower, the men were getting closer, and the motor sounded like it was getting asthma. "No, NO!" Neil screamed angrily.

Then one of the bullets hit their bright yellow boat. "Haku, put on the life vest and gimme one," Neil commanded.

This was it. Neil felt overwhelming fear. The boat was barely moving and the water was taking over. The life vests had blinkers but these maniacs were gonna find them and kill them.

The water was icy, Neil thought ruefully, so cold for such a warm place. He pulled Haku over and attached a cord to his jacket so they wouldn't lose each other in the inky blackness of the night waves. Finally, Neil took the bottle of water. This was it, they were in and losing the boat.

More bullets hit the water, then they saw the bad guys but their speed boat was turning away—someone else was firing at the meth crew. Neil turned to see a boat approaching and he started to scream for help.

A blinding light focused on Haku and Neil, "We see you," someone said over a loudspeaker, and then like the hands of heaven, two guys were pulling them to safety.

"Oh my God, oh my God," Neil kept repeating. "How did you find us?" He was panting—he really had thought he was going to die.

The guy with the bushy hair put a big towel around him. "Your big sister."

Neil put his head in his hands, he didn't want to cry, but when you're that close to a murky, watery, shark-chomping, sharpshooting death, some tears are in order.

The bullets were still flying but the meth posse was in retreat.

"They're probably going to try to remove all the product, ASAP," Sergeant Campbell said to them. "I'm gonna radio our backup."

"Who's the back up?" Neil asked carefully, worried the police were now involved.

The two military guys smiled at each other. "Oh, between Tuna's friends and your wife and sister you have quite a team."

"Tuna?" Neil said in shock.

Smyth explained the plan while he bandaged up the brave Haku. "This kid is solid," Neil explained, with an odd sense of pride.

"Your father will be happy to see you. He has the boat," Campbell said to a now-nervous kid.

As they all approached the pier, a lone man stood waiting to help them.

Campbell and Smyth rattled off the situation to the great dark man, who had a strange frog skeleton tattoo on his bulging bicep that was exposed in the harbor light, as he began tying up the boat. He spoke only to Smyth and Campbell. "Looks like we're going to have to go in under the cover of darkness. My crew can handle that." The man smiled, his teeth white in the dark, and he was gone before Neil could thank him.

Campbell addressed Neil. "We can fill you in after we get this guy home," he said, patting a relieved Haku on the soggy shoulder of his stained blue polo shirt.

"I hope my dad doesn't kick my ass," Huku said sheepishly.

"Well, I'd do some major butt-kissing and apologizing, if I were you," Neil recommended.

"Will do." Haku gave him a hug again. In a small way for a moment Neil wondered what it would be like to have a kid of his own.

"I'll try and look ya up before I leave. I'll put in a good word to your dad."

Jenny was crying, like he'd never seen her cry. He felt so awful he had made such a shitty decision, but hey, who knew?

Jenny, his sister, and some weird Asian dude in neon green sweats were all there to greet him back at the hotel.

They ordered some breakfast at a little café and the story unfolded.

"So wait, your comic book buddy Tuna got this hot shit biker guy, who's some Black Ops paramilitary man, to assemble a team to go bust these assholes?"

Lucy and Jenny replied at the same time, "Yes." They smirked at each other, relieved for the reality of this moment. Somehow everyone was safe and sound.

Between bites of her feta-and-spinach omelet Lucy elaborated. "Tuna told me he had a friend on Kwaj who he rode with when he was in town. We talked about you going to Kwaj. So I remembered that . . . then Jimmie Jay is the guy I'm renting my liveaboard from." Lucy nodded to Jimmie Jay, who was busy wolfing down his banana-mango waffle. "He's a retired cop."

"I pretty much found you," Jimmie Jay added, his modesty denied. "But I'm no Lone Ranger, I knew we needed help," his modesty reapplied.

"So what are these Hawaiian guys, and Black Ops Navy SEAL people gonna do? Are they going back to Disappearing Island?" Neil asked.

Jenny put down her coffee cup. "I'd leave that bit to them."

They all nodded.

The waitress was not so thrilled to be waiting on them so early, and she snorted in the background. She may have had a quieter morning in mind. "Need anything else?" she asked curtly.

They all declined.

Chapter 17

A moldy bed never felt so good as Lucy laid her weary bones to rest. She looked at her phone and realized she had never called Taylor back, let alone Amanda!

Lucy had a momentary panic attack when she saw a slew of missed messages on her phone. Amanda had no idea what had transpired in just three days, wait until she hears about this, Lucy thought. Then her head went back to her flat pillow and she allowed her body to ease up for the first time in days. She needed to rest just a little bit before they took off for the airport.

Jimmie Jay was back to snoring. He'd worked out alright. His sense of humor was just her speed too. In just a few hours she'd be back in Oahu. She was so glad everything had worked out safely. Maybe now she could get back to relaxing.

Another beautiful blue Hawaiian sky escorted Jimmie Jay and Lucy as they drove in Neil's hot rod through the streets of Honolulu. It was so strange to her how this place felt so much like home. Maybe if she made some money from this Martin deal she'd buy a little condo on Deep East . . . her favorite spot on the island . . . Hauula. She'd really not traveled that much, but Sshe liked being close to her brother.

"When you gonna call that fine singer chick?" Jimmie Jay asked, downshifting as they sped past countless little shops.

Islanders just going about their business, because for them, this was just another day in paradise in paradise.

"As soon as I get back to the boat. I'm kind of nervous." She felt the need to change the subject. "Hey, I meant to ask you what's up with that really, really old guy in the boat next to yours? He seems like an interesting fellow. The Tube Top Lady introduced us. I mean, did he really work for The Duke of Windsor and Doris Duke?, but quiet. Is he British?"

"He was Double Duked…hit by the dukey," Jimmie Jay was laughing at his own play on words. When I wasn't falling over with laughter he explained. "Yeah…he's legit. His parents actually worked for The Duke, he was just a kid. It was when King Edward was like the head honcho in the Bahama's… Dukey didn't like it and was out of there pretty fast. Then they guys family came to Oahu… you think Doris didn't want to hire someone who worked for British royalty…hell yes she did, cause she thought she was American royalty. She left him some dough and that's how he got the boat. He does charters now."

Lucy found all this very interesting. Life really was six degrees of separation.

Lucy and Jimmie Jay screeched into the parking spot by the marina and Jimmie Jay cut the engine. "Yeah, he's interesting all right. He grew up in the Bahamas and his folks worked for the Duke and Duchess of Windsor. Only gets talking when his pie-eyed, you'd dig him. Sometimes you can get him to talk, but he's not real social. I find him straight up weird. After Doris Duke croaked he started the charters. Too much time out at sea, he was a captain for these little tour boats out in the Marquesas Islands, *remote*. There's like still cannibals and shit out there, ya know. "

Jimmie Jay was heading to La Mariana and it was here where they parted company to his car, talking and walking. "You owe me some money and some dinner. I see you tonight at **Sorabol**. You drive, I want to get drunk!"

"Are you gonna meet me . . . here?" she asked. "Yeah…oh, let me get something outta my ride."

He jogged back to unlocked the door to the ugliest rust bucket she had ever seen. Jimmie Jay's car, a rusty repainted Yugo.

"Yeah, meet you on MY boat, I bring you a Fresca, make sure you got some cold beers for me."

She looked at the burnt orange car, dents revealing that the prior owner had painted it glow-in-the-dark orange. "Dude, I didn't even know any of these golf carts were still in existence!"

He sat in his Serbian mistake and gave her a smug grin. "Don't knock the ride—I own a yacht." He winked. "Now back to our agreement. I delivered. Now you don't try to welsh on a deal. I always get paid, I got this car playing poker."

Rolling her eyes dramatically, she replied, "Winning?" She smirked back as she waved him off.

He was a smart-ass but she liked him.

The boat was hot and muggy when she got back so she turned on the little air conditioner and prepared for a lackluster but much-needed shower. She was glad she brought what Amanda called her Jamaican muumuu. It was knee-length African print dashiki in vibrant, red, brown and blue. It made her think of her dad. There was a cute picture of him floating around in a very similar shirt on a fishing boat in Michigan, with a Hamm's beer raised high toasting to good times, smiling from behind his 1970s aviator glasses.

After she showered, she walked out to the deck of the boat, looking at the endless blue sky, and said, "I got him back, Dad, he's safe and sound."

She turned back around only to see the old guy next door looking at her curiously. There's an old saying, "It takes one to know one." He had that look of a life well lived with his slitty eyes, his rawhide skin, and his full head of white hair tucked beneath a well-worn army green Greek fisherman's cap. Lucy was younger but she'd unquestionably lived quite a full life herself. They nodded at each other but she needed to make some phone calls.

First call her saintly wife Amanda. Lucy just prayed she wasn't pissed that she'd been MIA. The phone rang and rang. Finally, Amanda picked up.

"I am so, so sorry," were the first words out of Amanda's mouth.

"What are you talking about?" Lucy almost dropped the phone.

"Didn't you hear my message? Someone stole my phone, right off my desk at the university. I've been using my backup flip phone but I can't get into the messages and I can't text. Then for some reason I tried calling you again and it kept dropping my calls."

Lucy laughed out loud.

"Is your brother OK? Are you feeling relaxed? I'm sure that Hawaiian sunshine and hanging ten is making all your cares melt away." Amanda had no idea. . . .

"Well, let's just say it's been a real whirlwind here." Lucy proceeded to explain the whole story to a shocked Amanda. There wwas a lot of "What!" "Oh my God," and "I can't believe what you are telling me."

"But wait, it gets better. When we're getting chased by the meth gang, Martin—ya know, THE Ashly Martin—she's FaceTiming me! Needless to say I didn't pick up." Lucy explained how Martin wanted to record a CD of all her songs. "Amanda . . . Amanda, are you there?"

Amanda's voice was muffled. "I just dropped the fucking phone, I can't process all this. I mean, only you, only you could have all this happen, Lucy." Amanda just kept making surprised sounds. "I want you to pause and remember all those tears and all that bitching"—she was quoting Lucy here—"*no one will ever hear my songs . . .* our country is a political rat's nest and I'm writing all this great stuff and only a bunch of drunks at the Houndstooth are gonna hear it," Amanda mimicked Lucy's self-pity pot whining. " The Suck Job lady likes it." Lucy had cried these very words, the notorious Suck Job lady was what the loggers called the local lady for hire who was a regular at the bar.

For almost a year Lucy had quit playing or singing her songs. The salon had been her salvation, allowing her to just throw herself into her new business. It was not quite as fulfilling as writing books or putting together an album, but it was reality.

Here was a new reality and a new chance to come full circle.

"Well, Lucy, I suggest you give this girl a call so I can become a kept woman," Amanda laughed.

"Next call!"

Chapter 18

Lucy made her way to the **Halekulani Hotel**, which had her favorite brunch in Hawaii. She was guided to a roped-off section on the veranda overlooking the ocean and Waikiki Beach. She had sat in this very spot, minus the ropes, a month after her dad had died. She and her brother had sipped fresh guava juice and Bloody Marys, wondering what the next step was going to be. He would soon be losing his house, to an ugly court battle involving his mortgage and their stepmother. Lucy was taking over the hair salon in Fossil Creek.

Now here was Lucy, just a few years later and on solid ground meeting one of the most famous pop stars in the country. Sometimes karma is a sweet kiss on the cheek.

The breeze was warmer than expected and Ashly was late. Lucy had a coffee and her journal. She had actually crammed a **Noah Van Sciver** comic into her oversized purse to remind herself of who she was—just a girl trying to navigate through life the best she knew how and find a little humor on the way.

Suddenly she realized the tables around her seemed to be peppered with men and women who didn't look like legit travelers. They were security. Their too-tight shoes, dark colors, and uptight demeanor gave them away.

Finally in swept Ashly, with what looked like her manager and a few other people. Luckily they went to other tables and Ashly made her way down to Lucy.

Lucy stood up and realized she had butterflies in her stomach. She also felt underdressed and fat. When she attempted to shake Ashly's hand Ashly pulled her in for a big hug "I'm a hugger!" Ashly explained as she pulled out her own seat and sat down. "This place is beautiful. No wonder you wanted to meet here."

Ashly was in a wispy pastel wrap dress, looking like a delicate bouquet of flowers. She was pale and taller than Lucy had expected and was rail thin. Her hair was long and blown out, pulled away from her face in a completely frizzless ponytail. Lucy straightened up as a few photographers attempted to flutter around them, trying to be un-intrusive as they took photos from all different angles. Lucy began to stiffen. She really wasn't up for this—this part of their meeting had not occurred to her.

Ashly realized Lucy's discomfort. "Sorry, hon, it's all part of the business. Social media. Just try to ignore them."

"It's so nice to meet you. I have to say this all feels very surreal to me."

"I know, it's crazy, right? But when I heard your songs I just knew you would be the one to help me really change my direction musically."

"What does that mean, really—"

Ashly paused and took a sip of her sparkling water. "Well, I want a new, more mature sound and image. I'm going to cut right to the chase here. Guy said you would be OK with me kind of polishing up your songs. I mean, I love the hooks and the lyrics, but —"

"The production could be more polished," Lucy cut in. Ashly's eyes grew wide. "Um, yes . . . yes."

Lucy said,   "I've listened to your last two albums, which were my favorite."

"Really? Because *Destructive Tendencies* wasn't a strong charter. . . ."

Lucy felt shockingly in her element. If there was one thing she knew it was music. "ItTt wasn't teenybopper pop, you dug deep, maybe a little on the sour grapes side . . . disappointment with the industry."

Lucy knew there were some songs directed at this other pop star who Ashly was feuding with and she had just changed agents.

"I really thought people would like it better," Ashly said in a moment of candor.

"To be honest, I wasn't a huge fan of yours until the last two albums. I mean, I know I'm not your demographic—teenage girls are. —I hope you can capture a more mature audience with my music, but it's going tonna take a lot to draw in a whole new fan base. Plus, my stuff is pretty hard hitting. I don't know if people want that stuff right now."

Ashly looked at Lucy hard. "I think you are modern-day Bob Dylan," She said. Her big baby-blue eyes suddenly looked very much like the letter of authority and it was Lucy who felt like the child.

Lucy almost choked. "My brother would love to hear you say that—he worships him," Lucy laughed. "But no one wants to hear Bob Dylan-style social/political struggle songs anymore. Dylan is a cozy memory of a time that has passed, people love nostalgia—Woodstock and tie-dyes. It's all merchandizing now."

"Let's order, shall we?" Ashly suggested.

It then occurred to Lucy they couldn't just go up to the buffet —when Lucy turned her chair around, a room full of people had their eyes and their phones trained on Ashly Martin. She turned back around and ordered the macadamia nut pancakes, knowing that there were a lot more tasty choices up there but they needed to stay roped in. It was a very strange feeling.

After their food came Ashly pulled out her phone and said, "You eat and listen to this."

From her jewel-encrusted phone came "Black Mirror" and "Virtual Life," two of Lucy's songs. But they sounded radically different. Ashly looked at her pensively while Lucy listened intently.

Lucy wiped her mouth and took a sip of her coffee. "These are so much better," she said with heartfelt awe. "I knew my lyrics and the hooks, like you said, were good, but I knew they were missing something . . . a key ingredient, and that is . . . you."

Ashly popped up and gave Lucy a hug. It all felt unreal, and yet it was the moment of vindication. It took this stranger, a musician she wasn't even a fan of, to give her songs the magic they were missing. It wasn't even hard to admit because Lucy was a fan of pop music first—and Ashly hadn't gotten to where she was because she was an idiot.

They talked until the afternoon sun began to make its way into evening. Lucy was so over-caffeinated she felt like she could backstroke all the way back to the boat.

Before they parted Lucy added, "I think it's so ironic that this is probably the first time in my life I have found another woman to talk about music with. Isn't that sad?"

"Well, I don't think that will be the case anymore. Oh, there is one song I'm not recording, it doesn't fit with the vibe of the album or my voice."

"Which one?" Lucy asked curiously.

"'Your Daughter.' It's a blues song and should be recorded at a blues label. So if it's OK with you, I talked to some guys at Crocodile Records in Chicago, they'll record it. If you want you can work on some songs to go with it, release an EP, I'll support it."

Lucy thought about what a smart move this was. Lucy would not be competition in this genre, she would be indebted to Ashly, and it would be easier for Lucy to succeed in blues than pop music.

"I'll think about it," was her answer. Lucy was kind of relieved to not have to chase the music dragon. She'd talk to Amanda and make decisions later . . . after her, um, vacation.

The valets brought her brother's Firebird around with its obnoxiously loud pipes. Bentleys, Benzes, and Maseratis were pulling up and yet a cocky proud little buzz filled her chest. It had finally paid off to be the weirdo she couldn't stop being, even if she tried.

Chapter 19

Lucy couldn't sleep. She had tossed and turned all night. Her mind was buzzing with all the recent events. It almost felt like after a concert when she'd sat too close to the speakers and her whole body was still vibrating with sensory overload.

She decided to brew some coffee and take a long drive down to the Magnum Beach, as she liked to call it. For some reason Waimanalo just seemed reassuring. She could watch the sun come up.

She wiggled into her bathing suit, stretchy cotton shorts, and a Blues Brothers T-shirt. She thought the choice was ironic.

As she flipped off all the lights on the boat except for one so she could make her way off, she noticed the British Guy was up. She could see him smoking and fixing a fishing line. She swore he nodded her way and went back to his mending. She wished she was more still, that she could just sit in the dark watching the world come awake, but she was just too antsy.

Hopefully the car didn't wake anyone up, she thought, as she got on the highway, thanking her lucky stars for GPS.

It was mostly military folks working the early shift who seemed to be out and about when she got on Kam Highway. it was quieter, and she made her way alongside the ocean between the mountains. She hoped Neil never moved from here—she loved Oahu so very much.

When she finally saw the familiar road and turned into the little parking lot there were just a couple of pickup trucks, probably belonging to the guys who were out fishing. It was still pretty dark and the blinking blue and green lights beyond the tidal pool reminded her of when she met Tuna, and his comment to her that if she swam past the tidal pool she could be shark bait. No thanks! Yet here were these native guys fishing nightly, nary one shark chomp!

The water still looked a little ominous at this time before dawn. She waded over the slippery jagged rocks alongside the high seawall, making her way to the little cove of sand and beach by the rotting cottage that would soon be torn down to make way for the new owners of the old 1980s *Magnum P.I.* property. A cold wave splashed her crotch and she was stunned awake. She lifted her chair and backpack, trying to keep them dry. She was looking forward to her thermos of hot coffee. Something bumped against her leg and she scrambled, almost falling face forward onto the little cut of beach. Erosion had drunk up most of her favorite spot, the ocean turning a coastal inlet to a small three-chair patch of sand and rocks.

Setting up her chair, she positioned herself as some might for a spectator sport, but her main event was the sunrise.

As she got comfortable in her chair, she began digging out her ancient iPod. She thought about the day ahead. Neil was taking all of them out tonight—Tuna and Ailani, the Black Ops guy, and all the spouses—to Ruth's Chris. It would be a hefty tab but in the scheme of things it was a small price to pay for being alive.

"Kinda risky coming out here in the dark, you almost took a header on the rocks!"

She yelped in fear, almost falling out of her seat. In the dusk she could see an older man with a cowboy-type hat and some round academic-looking spectacles. She recognized him as he walked down from the opening by the gate along the seawall that led up to the Magnum House.

"Aren't you Jack Knivves?" she asked.

"Yes, and you might be . . . ?"

"Lucy Zwick." She felt like she should submit a résumé to him and explain why she was worthy of this conversation.

He said, "I think I've seen you before. Your name rings a bell."

She snorted, "Well, actually, I sent you a song a while back . . . about um, your work."

"Ohhhh, yes."

He didn't sound too impressed so she started to defend herself.

"I know it's probably not you're normal listening fare, but the song was composed of almost all the titles of your books, and yet it tells the story of my life, and yours sort of, too."

"I kind of got that."

There was an awkward silence. She scratched her neck. Prickles of the first rays of morning sunlight were illuminating the beach.

She started to ramble nervously, "I'm from Chicago, moved to a small town outside of Montreal, Canada, and my brother lives here . . . for many years now."

"Yes, I've seen you around, um, you're hard to miss," he said, nodding toward her big bush of curly blond hair and trademark white glasses.

"Do you live here?" Lucy asked, nodding toward the house.

"   Oh, heavens no, I've done well for myself, but not quiet Robin Masters rich."

"Haha," she laughed at the TV show reference.

"I'm house sitting, I guess you'd call it. The Robinsons are out of town and my house is being fumigated—while I was on Cape Cod, some critters settled into my place up in the hills and now it's going to be a week before I can return."

"Ahhh." Lucy figured she might as well go for it and ask for a tour. "I heard they are tearing this place down. . . ."

"They are, it's been sold."

"Any chance you could give me a tour? This may sound weird, but this house is very sentimental to me."

He thought for a second. Lucy knew he didn't want to, so she was surprised when he said yes.

"All right, follow me, I'd take your things, though. Lots of theft around here," he explained, leading the way beyond the rusty gates Lucy had longed to pass through all her life.

The tennis courts were overgrown to the point of being indistinguishable from the rocky rubble. Weeds and leaves had grown between the old, green, formerly opulent asphalt foundation, and the netting had dissolved into a snarly tangled moldy mess.

She could not believe she was walking on this property with one of her all-time favorite authors. On the other hand, her stomach fell as she saw how dilapidated the former white mansion by the sea looked. Originally it has been white stucco and concrete with beautiful foliage and blooming flowers. Now, the walls of the house were deeply pocked with age, mold scarred the exterior walls like green veiny skin, and little plants grew out of some of the deeper cracks in the facade. Window frames were weather beaten and rotting, and the wrought iron on the second-floor balconies off the bedrooms looked rusty and dangerous.

The grandeur of the foyer was still very old Hollywood. It reminded her a kind of Spanish colonial rustic design. She could imagine Errol Flynn in a seersucker suit, tossing his riding hat on the table and pouring himself a tumbler of bourbon and then flopping down on the big dark leather couches in the main library sitting area off the front of the house.

"It's not the grand manse that it used to be but it still has one of the best views on the island," Jack added, as he stood behind Lucy, letting her take in all the details.

The fixtures were so dated, all dark bronze, the oriental rugs were worn through, and the books had begun to disintegrate and molder as they stood bravely on their dark wood bookcases, knowing their time for retirement was near. A few cardboard boxes were already partly filled with relics from the shelves.

In another working office, a sort of beachy 1980s flair was more apparent with brass-and-glass shelves, little knickknacks from travels carelessly displayed like an afterthought. A boombox was sitting on a little TV table behind a less impressive off-white desk, and next to it an old electric typewriter and a clunky laptop were almost buried among piles of bills, tablets of paper, letters, and post-it notes. The paneled walls reminded her of a 1970s basement.

Jack broke the silence. "Would you like a bottle of water?"

"Yes, actually, that would be great."

"It lacks the former glory of your fantasy?" Jack asked.

As they made their way upstairs she was shocked he was being so accommodating.

The grand master bedroom was almost empty. Obviously the owners had finished emptying this room first. As she walked toward the opulent French doors toward the view of a lifetime, she almost gasped. She wished feverishly she was a millionaire so she could buy this house and refurbish it to its deserving historical significance.

"I always wanted to ask someone . . . um . . . a fan, why all the reverence toward this seemingly banal television show?" Jack asked with a hint of scorn.

She looked beyond the lush trees at the electric-blue ocean, its white foamy waves rocking animatedly, pushing around boats and swimmers, an ocean alive with expectation. She wondered how she could ever explain that this silly show had gotten her all the way from Hohman, Indiana, to paradise.

"It wasn't really the show so much as how it brought my very dysfunctional family together and we all dreamed the same dream in our own unique way, for one hour, a week. It was during the height of my father's business success and the future looked so bright. We all had these raging high hopes. The show distracted us from the reality of who we really were and made us feel hopeful and excited, like we could be or go anywhere we wanted, and life would be cool."

"Things turned out differently."

"Oh yes," Lucy laughed. It was too much to explain and Jack seemed to understand. "But, Jack, it got me here, talking to a world-renowned author, selling my songs and running a business back in Canada, solving my own life mysteries and adventures much like good old Magnum—pretty impressive for a bushy-haired nerd from Northwest Indiana."

"I'd say so," he smiled, checking his watch.

"Thanks for the tour, I'll never forget it."

"Thanks for the song. It meant something," he said almost tenderly, " . . . sorry I never sent a thank-you."

As they made their way back outside and he showed her to the gate, he nodded, adjusting his glasses. "Maybe I'll see you around," Lucy said obligingly.

"Like I said, you stand out."

They both had a good laugh and she made her way back to the beach.

Cries of families and folks having a good time swimming and picnicking greeted her. She went in for one last dip. Next time she came back this place would be demo'd—gone, with only her memories remaining.

Life would move forward, like it or not. The future would be coming and Lucy had decided to embrace it for all it was worth. She got on her knees, looking out over the endless blue, and said a prayer of thanks to "the Big Guy." Then she waded into the tidal pool. This would probably be her last swim here.

There were other beaches and places to explore. Her memories would always be alive in her heart.

Damn, if her life wasn't a real-life episode of her own version of *Magnum*!

Chapter 20

Honolulu Police Dept.
801 S. Beretania, Honolulu, HI
Sgt. Ken Laguna and Sgt. Andy Koike, 4:45 a.m.

The office smelled of burnt coffee and Old Spice cologne. The sun had yet to make its morning appearance and confirm it was a new day.

"Morning, Laguna. You got Malasada powder on your tie," Sergeant Andy Koike said, still bleary eyed on his early-morning call, pouring himself a cup of burnt coffee.

"I brought that creamer." Sergeant Laguna pointed at the Sweet Cream Cinnabon Delight liquid creamer as he brushed the powdered sugar off his navy blue tie.

"Thanks, brah, cuts the taste of this sludge."

"I thought you was gonna quit with that stinky aftershave," Sergeant Koike said, taking his first swig of liquid sustenance.

"My lipo got it for me for my birthday. She won't like it if I don't wear it."

"Smell like my dad."

"Yeah, well, gotta keep my wahine happy. She's a good girl."

There was a pause in the rarely silent police break room. Koike checked his hair in the tarnished mirror and put on his duty cop cap. It had the Coolmax fabric liner and he was glad for it because today was gonna be a hot one.

"Hey, did you see that rusty old disgusting shrimp truck out front?"

"Hell, yeah, who would eat outta that bacteria mobile? Some unsuspecting tourist, right?" They both chuckled and shook their heads.

"Stop talking about it, you're making me sick, brudda."

At about 5:30 Laguna and Koike were ready to go on patrol. When they pulled their car around the sun was just hitting the Big Kahuna Shrimp Truck.

"Is it just me or something doesn't look right about that truck?"

"It's too gross, brah, no one should be eating there. It almost looks abandoned."

"Let's take a look." They nodded in unison.

The two officers exited their squad car. The truck didn't even look drivable, the rust had almost consumed its outer carriage, the tires were practically flat, and the smiling shrimp that had once advertised Mahalo Scampi was a faded husk of corrosion with only one smiling eye discernible.

Then came the thud from with the truck.

Both officers stepped back. They looked at each other and drew their service revolvers. "Honolulu Police Department. Please exit the vehicle, I repeat, please exit the vehicle."

More vicious thudding.

"We should call this in." Laguna radioed that they were attempting to open an abandoned vehicle with a possible occupant inside.

A few minutes later they had a crowbar and backup.

When they popped the lock no one could believe their eyes. Three men and a very psychotic-looking woman were tied up with stacks of what looked to be packages of drugs and paraphernalia for making methamphetamines.

All Sergeant Koike could say under his breath was, "What the fuck?"

At 500 Ala Moana Boulevard at a big cozy table in back, Neil was treating everyone to a big juicy rib eye at Ruth's Chris Steak House.

Jenny was a vegetarian so she got the creamed spinach, fresh broccoli, and Cremini mushrooms. Tuna and Margo were splitting a New York Strip, Jimmie Jay was still salivating over his beef choices and ordering another beer, Sergeants Campbell and Smyth sent their regards but were on duty, but the star of the evening, Ailani, their Pacific Island Black Ops angel, was remaining quiet as he sipped his whiskey and decided on the Chilean sea bass.

Amanda had taken the next plane out of Montreal as soon as she heard the story. She had joined the group, never one to miss a good steak! Jimmie Jay toyed with the idea of charging extra for two rescues, "I was only hired to get your brotha' that local kid should be extra," he joked. guests but thought better of it since Neil had offered to pay the wages he lost at the bar when he helped Lucy track Neil and Haku down.

"Ailani, what ended up happening to the drug dealers?" Amanda asked, nibbling on her lettuce wedge smothered in Blue Cheese dressing.

He smiled a wide, white-toothed grin that the Cheshire Cat would've been proud of and took another deep sip of his Maker's Mark. "Let's just say they're right where they belong."

Jimmie Jay added, "I hear through the grapevine some funky shrimp got disposed of at HPD doorstep . . . dat's nice for them." Jimmie gave Ailani a sly look and popped another piece of calamari in his mouth.

"Bad shrimp is an awful thing," Ailani said, nodding. "Bacteria, parasites can contaminate the gut . . . makes everyone sick. Gotta take care of those infections."

Lucy smiled and looked around the table. They all seemed to understand perfectly.

The main course arrived and Neil had another announcement—or three. "You know how much I love Oahu," he began, "but you also know how expensive it is to live here. So good news and sad news. We found a great house on the Big Island and Jenny has been promoted with the ability to work from home! I am also the proud lessee of a gently used 1985 Cessna Caravan II prop plane, ready for inner island shuttles, thanks to my neighbor who is gifting it to me until he gets out of the pen for tax evasion." Neil explained to Lucy in private that the guy from the yellow mansion up the street needed to insure he had some dough after he did his time…that's what the sparkly rocks were for that had been so ceremoniously dropped off. "That DeLorean was auctioned off the day after you saw him." Neil added when she asked about the car.

Everyone applauded, but with different levels of confidence in these new revelations.
Lucy knowing her brother as she did, knew another strange family vacation would be lurking around the corner next year.

The waiter came over to the table with champagne for them and a gift bag for Lucy.

"Who is that is from?" Neil asked Lucy.

She shrugged.

The waiter began pouring champagne and explained.
"There's a note attached to the on the gift bag."

Lucy could feel it was something breakable, so she delicately unfolded the tissue paper, a smile spreading across her face.

"What is it?" Jimmie Jay said impatiently. "c'mon, let see."

She showed everyone at the table. They were all mystified, except her brother and Amanda.

The card read, "*Good luck on your adventures. I found this cleaning out the house and thought you would appreciate it,*" Sincerely, Jack Knivves.

"It's ugly mug?" Jimmie Jay commented. "Why you so happy?"

"Jimmie, it's a Magnum P.I. tiki mug, from Jack Knivves, the author."

"Ohhh, see it's always something stupid with you. . . ."

"Zip your lip, big guy, you're talking to my sister," Neil said, looking comically ominous.

Lucy looked around to see Jack Knivves and the English neighbor from Jimmie's boat heading out the front door of the restaurant. She thought about running after them but she had a feeling they'd meet again.